CRITICAL ACCLAIM FOR
MERLINE LOVELACE

"Merline Lovelace is the brightest new star in the romance genre. Each new book is an adventure."
—*New York Times* bestselling author
Debbie Macomber

"Ms. Lovelace delivers sizzling romantic adventure in the finest tradition and leaves us begging for more."
—*Romantic Times*, on *Night of the Jaguar*, from the original CODE NAME: DANGER miniseries

"You won't want to wait for the next book in this four-part series!"
—*The Paperback Forum*, on the original CODE NAME: DANGER miniseries

"…One of the best dramatic and heart-throbbing miniseries to hit the bookshelves in ages."
—*Affaire de Coeur*, on the original CODE NAME: DANGER miniseries

"Full of spine-tingling adventure à la James Bond, but Ms. Lovelace doesn't let that overshadow the tension-filled romance."
—*Genie Romance Exchange*, on *Perfect Double*, from the original CODE NAME: DANGER miniseries

Dear Reader,

It's August, and our books are as hot as the weather, so if it's romantic excitement you crave, look no further. Merline Lovelace is back with the newest CODE NAME: DANGER title, *Texas Hero*. Reunion romances are always compelling, because emotions run high. Add the spice of danger and you've got the perfection of the relationship between Omega agent Jack Carstairs and heroine-in-danger Ellie Alazar.

ROMANCING THE CROWN continues with Carla Cassidy's *Secrets of a Pregnant Princess*, a marriage-of-convenience story featuring Tamiri princess Samira Kamal and her mysterious bodyguard bridegroom. Marie Ferrarella brings us another of THE BACHELORS OF BLAIR MEMORIAL in *M.D. Most Wanted*, giving the phrase "doctor-patient confidentiality" a whole new meaning. Award-winning New Zealander Frances Housden makes her second appearance in the line with *Love Under Fire*, and her fellow Kiwi Laurey Bright checks in with *Shadowing Shahna*. Finally, wrap up the month with Jenna Mills and her latest, *When Night Falls*.

Next month, return to Intimate Moments for more fabulous reading—including the newest from bestselling author Sharon Sala, *The Way to Yesterday*. Until then…enjoy!

Yours,

Leslie J. Wainger

Leslie J. Wainger
Executive Senior Editor

Please address questions and book requests to:
Silhouette Reader Service
U.S.: 3010 Walden Ave., P.O. Box 1325, Buffalo, NY 14269
Canadian: P.O. Box 609, Fort Erie, Ont. L2A 5X3

MERLINE LOVELACE
Texas Hero

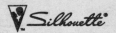

INTIMATE MOMENTS™

Published by Silhouette Books

America's Publisher of Contemporary Romance

SILHOUETTE BOOKS

ISBN 0-373-27235-9

TEXAS HERO

Copyright © 2002 by Merline Lovelace

MERLINE LOVELACE

spent twenty-three years as an Air Force officer, serving tours at the Pentagon and at bases all over the world before she began a new career as a novelist. When she's not tied to her keyboard, this RITA® Award-winning author and her husband of thirty years, Al, enjoy traveling, golf and long lively dinners with friends and family. Be sure to watch for *Once a Hero,* the next in the CODE NAME: DANGER miniseries, in Intimate Moments.

Merline enjoys hearing from readers and can be reached through Harlequin's Web site at www.eHarlequin.com.

This book is dedicated to my own handsome hero,
who I first met in the shadow of the Alamo.
Many thanks for all those wonderful
San Antonio memories, my darling.

Prologue

"Thank God for air-conditioning!"

Swiping a forearm across his dirt-streaked forehead, the tall, flame-haired grad student followed his team leader into the welcoming coolness of San Antonio's Menger Hotel.

"If I'd had any idea how muggy it gets down here in July," he grumbled, "I wouldn't have let you talk me into assisting you on this project."

"Funny," the woman beside him responded with a smile, "I seem to recall a certain Ph.D. candidate *begging* me to let him in on the dig."

"Yeah, well, that was before I realized I'd be branded as a defiler of history and practically run out of Texas on a rail."

Elena Maria Alazar's smile faded. Frowning, she shifted the strap of her heavy field case from one aching shoulder to the other and stabbed at the elevator buttons. Eric's complaints weren't all that exaggerated. He and everyone else working the project had come under increasingly vitriolic fire in recent days.

Dammit, she shouldn't have allowed the media to poke around the archeological site, much less elicit a hypothesis as to the identity of the remains found in the creek bed. She was an expert in her field, a respected member of the American Society of Forensic Historians, for pity's sake! She headed a highly skilled team of anthropologists and archeologists. She knew better than to let her people discuss their initial findings with reporters. Particularly when those findings held such potentially explosive local significance.

She couldn't blame anyone but herself for the howls of outrage that rose when the *San Antonio Express-News* reported that Dr. Elena Alazar, niece of Mexico's President Alazar and professor of history at the University of Mexico, was rewriting Texas history. According to the story, Ellie had found proof that legendary William Barrett Travis, commander of the Texans at the Alamo, hadn't died heroically with his men as always believed. Instead, he'd run away from the battle, was hunted down by Santa Anna's troops and was shot in back like a yellow, craven coward.

Ellie and her team were a long way yet from *proving* anything, but try telling that to the media! The *Express-News* wasn't any more interested in running a disclaimer than a correction to identify her as a professor of history at the University of *New* Mexico. Never mind that Ellie had been born and raised in the States. To the reporter's mind—and to the minds of his readers—she was an outsider attempting to mess with Texas history.

Thoroughly disgruntled, she made another stab at the brass-caged elevator. It was an antique, like everything else in the hundred-year-old hotel located just steps from the Alamo. Until the story broke, Ellie had thoroughly enjoyed her stay at the luxuriously appointed establishment. Now, she felt the weight of disapproval from every employee at the hotel, from desk clerks to the maid who cleaned her room.

She didn't realize just how much she'd earned the locals' displeasure, however, until she unlocked the door to her suite. Startled, she stopped dead. Behind her, Eric let out a long, low whistle.

"Folks around here sure let you know when they're not happy. I haven't seen a room trashed this bad since pledge week at the frat house. Come to think of it, I've *never* seen a room trashed this bad."

The two-room suite hadn't been just trashed, Ellie soon discovered. It had been ransacked. Her laptop

computer was gone, as was the external drive that
stored the data and thousands of digital images her
team had collected to date.

The loss of her equipment was bad enough, but
the message scrawled across the mirror above the
dresser made her skin crawl.

Mexican bitch.
I've got you in my crosshairs.
Get the hell out of Texas!

Chapter 1

Washington, D.C., steamed in the late afternoon July heat. On a quiet side street just off Massachusetts Avenue, in the heart of the embassy district, the chestnut trees drooped like tired old women and tar bubbled in the cracks of the sidewalk. The broad-shouldered man who emerged from a Yellow Cab took care not to step in the sticky blackness as he crossed the sidewalk and mounted the front steps of an elegant, Federal-style town house located midway down the block.

He paused for a moment, his gaze thoughtful as he studied the discreet bronze plaque beside the front door. The inscription on the plaque identified the three-story town house as home to the offices of the

President's special envoy. Most Washingtonians considered the special envoy's position a meaningless one, created years ago for a billionaire campaign contributor with a yen for a fancy title and an office in the nation's capital. Only a handful of insiders knew the special envoy also served as the head of a covert agency whose initials comprised the last letter of the Greek alphabet, OMEGA. An agency that, as its name implied, was activated only as a last resort in instances when other, more established organizations like the CIA or the Department of Defense couldn't respond for legal or practical reasons.

This was one of those instances.

Squaring his shoulders, the visitor entered the foyer and approached the receptionist seated behind a graceful Queen Ann desk.

"I am Colonel Luis Esteban. I'm here to see the special envoy."

"Oh, my! So you are."

Elizabeth Wells might have qualified for Medicare a number of years ago, but her hormones still sat up and took notice of a handsome man. And Colonel Luis Esteban, as OMEGA agent Maggie Sinclair had reported after a mission deep in the jungles of Central America, was gorgeous—drop-your-jaw, boggle-your-eyes gorgeous.

Elizabeth managed to keep her jaw from sagging, but the colonel's dark, melting eyes, pencil-thin black mustache and old-world charm did a serious number on her heart rate.

"I believe the special envoy is expecting me."

"What? Oh! Yes, of course. Mr. Jensen's in his office. With Chameleon, as you requested."

"Ah, yes." A small, private smile played about the colonel's mouth. "Chameleon."

Elizabeth's pulse tripped again, but not with pleasure this time. Having served as personal assistant to both Maggie *and* her husband, Adam Ridgeway, during their separate tenures as director of OMEGA, Elizabeth wouldn't hesitate to empty the Sig Sauer 9 mm tucked in her desk drawer into anyone who tried to come between them. With something very close to a sniff, she lifted the phone on her desk and buzzed her boss. Her gaze had cooled several degrees when she relayed his reply.

"Go right in, Colonel."

"Thank you."

Luis walked down a short hall, opened a door shielded from attack by a lining of Kevlar, took one step inside and plunged into chaos. There was an ear-shattering woof. A flash of blue and orange. A chorus of shouts.

"Dammit, he's doing it again."

"Radizwell! No!"

"Shut the door, man!"

A hissing, bug-eyed lizard the size of a small hound darted between Luis's legs. A second later, a huge sheepdog tried to follow. Knocked sideways, Luis grabbed the door handle while the furiously barking hound raced after the iguana. Doubling back, the lizard leaped for the safety of a polished mahogany conference table. Once there, it whipped out a foot-long tongue and spit at the jumping, madly woofing hound.

"Nick!" Half-laughing and wholly exasperated, Maggie Sinclair shouted an appeal to OMEGA's current director. "Get Radizwell out of here."

The man who answered her plea sported a lean, well-muscled body under his elegantly tailored suit, but it took all his strength to drag the vociferously protesting hound out of the office. Deep, mournful howls followed him when he returned. Closing the door to muffle the yowls, he smoothed his blond hair with a manicured hand and shot Luis a wry smile.

"Nick Jensen, Colonel. I'd apologize for the noisy reception, but…" He glanced at the still hissing giant iguana. "I understand you were the diabolical fiend who gave Maggie her pet in the first place."

"Yes, he was." A smile lighting her eyes, Maggie Sinclair came across the spacious office and held out both hands. "Hello, Luis. How are you?"

Esteban's gaze took in her glowing face, dropped to her gently rounded stomach. Regret punched through him. He'd had his chance with this woman a number of years ago. She slipped away from him then, as changeable and lightning quick as her code name implied.

Luis had come to Washington on urgent business at the request of the president of Mexico. Only he knew that he also brought with him the half-formed idea of reigniting the sparks that had once flared between Maggie and him. He'd heard she'd left OMEGA to finish writing a book and raise her two small daughters. He'd thought perhaps she might be bored and ready for a touch of excitement. He could see at a glance that wasn't the case, however. Maggie Sinclair wore the look of a woman well and truly loved.

Swallowing a small sigh, he lifted her hands and dropped a light kiss on the back of each. "I'm well, Chameleon. And you... You are as lively and beautiful as ever."

"I don't know about the beautiful part, but my family certainly keeps things lively." Rueful laughter filled her honey brown eyes. "I thought you might want to see how your gift has grown over the years. Unfortunately, Terence won't go anywhere these days without his buddy, the sheepdog you just met. They're best of pals until Radizwell, er, well..."

"Gets the hots for the damned thing," the third person in the room said. He strolled forward, his blue eyes keen in his aristocratic face. "Adam Ridgeway, colonel."

"Ah, yes," Luis drawled, returning both the

strong grip and rapierlike scrutiny. "Maggie's husband."

"Maggie's husband," he affirmed with a smile that sent an instant and unmistakable message. "Hope you don't mind if I sit in on your meeting. I'm told it involves one of the agents I recruited for OMEGA."

Instantly all business, Luis Esteban nodded. "Yes, it does. Jack Carstairs. I understand he's on his way to San Antonio."

"He left a few hours ago," Nick Jensen replied, gesturing the other three to seats well away from the conference table occupied by the wary, unblinking iguana. "What *we* don't understand, however, is how Renegade's mission concerns you."

"Allow me to explain. When I first met Chameleon, I was chief of security for my country. I've since retired and established my own firm. I do very private, very discreet work for a number of international clients. The President of Mexico is one of them. He asked me to run a background check on Jack Carstairs."

Nick's brows lifted. "Did he?"

"Yes. You know, of course, that Carstairs once had an affair with President Alazar's niece."

"We know. Which made us wonder why he requested Carstairs for this mission in the first place."

"He didn't, actually. The request came from his niece."

Flicking his shirt cuff over his gold Rolex, Luis picked his way through a potentially explosive international minefield.

"As you're aware, Elena's father—President Alazar's youngest brother—emigrated to the States as a young man. He and Ellie's mother met in Santa Fe and married after a whirlwind courtship. Unfortunately, Carlos Alazar died before his daughter was born, but his wife made sure Ellie spent summers with her father's family in Mexico. During one of those visits, Ellie met a Marine pulling guard duty at the U.S. Embassy. Their affair was brief and, I'm told, rather indiscreet."

"Indiscreet enough to get Gunnery Sergeant Carstairs sent home in disgrace and subsequently booted out of the Marines," Nick acknowledged.

"Evidently Ellie feels a lingering responsibility for ruining the man's military career. When her uncle decided she needed a bodyguard, she insisted it be Carstairs. Which is why President Alazar hired me to check him out."

"How did you get past Renegade's cover and make the link to OMEGA?" Nick asked, not liking the idea that one of his agents had been compromised.

Luis merely smiled. "I think Chameleon will attest that I, too, possess certain skills. Suffice to say I uncovered his connection to OMEGA and advised President Alazar, who subsequently made the call to your President, requesting Carstairs's services.''

''And now President Alazar's having second thoughts about the request?''

''Let's just say he's worried that Carstairs's past involvement with his niece might get in the way of his ability to maintain the detachment required for this job.''

Nick Jensen, code name Lightning, didn't for a second doubt Jack Carstairs's ability to do his job. During Nick's days as an operative, he'd gone into the field with Renegade more than once and had gained a profound respect for his skills. Nick also, however, possessed a Gallic understanding of the power of passion.

Once a skinny, perpetually hungry pickpocket who called the back streets of Cannes home, Henri Nicolas Everard had been adopted by Paige and Doc Jensen, moved to the States and had grown to manhood in a house filled with love. He'd parlayed the near starvation of his childhood into a string of high-priced restaurants scattered around the globe.

Nick was now a millionaire many times over. His cover as a jet-setter gave him access to the world of movie princes and oil sheikhs. It had also led to a number of discreet affairs with some of the world's most beautiful women. A true connoisseur, he could understand why Jack Carstairs had sacrificed his military career for a fling with Elena Maria Alazar. The background dossier compiled by OMEGA's chief of communications had painted a portrait of an astonishingly vibrant, incredibly intelligent woman.

Not unlike OMEGA's chief of communications herself, Nick thought. A mental image of Mackenzie Blair replaced that of Ellie Alazar and produced a sudden tightening just below his Italian leather belt. Both amused and perturbed by the sensation, Nick offered his assurances to Colonel Esteban.

"OMEGA wouldn't have sent Renegade into the field if we weren't absolutely confident in his ability to protect Dr. Alazar. If it will ease President Alazar's mind, however, I'll pass on his concerns."

"Perhaps you might also keep me apprised of the situation in San Antonio," Esteban suggested politely.

Everyone in the room recognized that they were treading tricky diplomatic ground here. Relations between the United States and Mexico had reached new, if somewhat shaky, levels with the recent North American Free Trade Association Treaty. The last thing either president wanted right now was an ugly international incident souring an economic agreement that had taken decades to hammer out.

"Not a problem," Nick said smoothly. "Once we ascertain that's what President Alazar wishes, of course."

"Of course." Rising, the colonel dug into his suit

pocket and produced a business card. "You can contact me day or night at this number."

His gaze drifted to Maggie, who rose and gave him a warm smile.

"Don't worry, Luis. Renegade's one of the best field operatives in the business. He wouldn't be working for OMEGA otherwise."

With that blithe assurance, she strolled across the office and clipped a leash on the unblinking iguana. Identical expressions of repulsion crossed the faces of Nick and the colonel as the creature's long tongue flicked her cheek in a quick, adoring kiss. Adam merely looked resigned.

"We'll walk you out," he said to Esteban. "Lightning has some calls to make."

OMEGA's acting director made the calls from the control center located on the third floor.

Mackenzie Blair ruled OMEGA's CC, just as she used to rule the command, control and communication centers aboard the Navy ships she'd served on. She loved this world of high-tech electronics, felt right at home in the soft green glow from the wall-size computer screens—far more at home than she'd ever felt in the two-bedroom condo she and her ex had once shared.

One of the problems was that she and David had never stayed in port together long enough to establish joint residency. He'd adjusted to the separations better than Mackenzie had, though. She discovered that when she returned two days early from a Caribbean cruise and found the jerk in bed with a neighbor's wife.

She'd sworn off men on the spot. Correction, she'd planted a very hard, very satisfying knee in David's groin when he'd grabbed her arm and tried to explain, *then* sworn off men.

Lately, though, she'd been reconsidering forever. Her itchy restlessness had nothing to do with her boss. Nothing at all. Just a woman's natural needs and the grudging realization that even the most sophisticated high-tech gadgets couldn't *quite* substitute for a man.

Which was why goose bumps raised all over her skin when Lightning strolled over to her command console with the casual grace that characterized him.

"Patch me through to the White House."

She cocked a brow. She wasn't in the Navy now.

"Please," Lightning added with an amused smile.

All too conscious of his proximity, Mackenzie transmitted the necessary code words and verifications, then listened with unabashed interest to the brief conversation between Lightning and the Prez. When it was over, she leaned back in her chair and angled OMEGA's director a curious look.

"Sounds like Renegade's got the weight of the free world riding on his shoulders on this one."

"The weight of North America, anyway."

His gaze lingered on her upturned face. Mackenzie had almost forgotten how to breathe by the time he murmured a request that she get Renegade on the line.

His eyes, narrowed and rattlesnake-mean behind his mirrored sunglasses, Jack Carstairs snapped shut the phone Mackenzie Blair had issued him mere hours ago. The damned thing was half the size of a cigarette pack and bounced signals off a secure tele-communications satellite some thirty-six thousand kilometers above the earth. Lightning's message had come through loud and clear.

Renegade was to keep his hands off Elena Maria Alazar.

As if he needed the warning! He'd learned his lesson the first time. No way was he going to get shot down in flames again.

Hefting his beat-up leather carryall, he walked out of the airport into a flood of heat and honeysuckle-scented air. A short tram ride took him to the rental agency, where he checked out a sturdy Jeep Chero-kee.

The drive from the airport to downtown San Antonio took only about fifteen minutes, long enough for Jack to work through his irritation at the call. Not long enough, however, to completely suppress the prickly sensation that crawled along his nerves at the thought of seeing Ellie Alazar again.

His jaw set, he negotiated the traffic in the city's center and pulled up at the Menger. Constructed in 1859, the hotel was situated on Alamo Plaza, right next to the famous mission. The little blurb Jack had read in one of the airline's magazines during the flight down indicated the Menger had played host to a roster of distinguished notables. Reportedly, Robert E. Lee rode his horse, Traveller, right into the lobby. Teddy Roosevelt tipped a few in the bar while organizing and training his Rough Riders. Sarah Bernhardt, Lillie Langtry and Mae West had all brought their own brand of luster to the hotel.

Now Elena Maria Alazar was adding another touch of notoriety to the venerable institution. One Jack suspected wasn't particularly appreciated by the management.

He killed the engine, then climbed out of the Cherokee. A valet took the car keys. Another offered to take his bag.

"I've got it."

Anyone else entering the hotel's three-story lobby for the first time might have let their gaze roam the cream marble columns, magnificent wrought-iron balcony railings and priceless antiques and paintings. Six years of embassy guard duty and another eight working for OMEGA had conditioned Jack to automatically note the lobby's physical layout, security camera placement and emergency egress routes. His boot heels echoing on the marble floors, he crossed to the desk. There he was handed a message. Ellie was waiting for him in the taproom.

After the blazing sun outside and dazzling white marble of the lobby, the bar wrapped Jack in the welcoming gloom of an English pub. A dark cherry-wood ceiling loomed above glass-fronted cabinets, beveled mirrors and high-backed booths. A stuffed moose head with a huge rack of antlers surveyed the scene with majestic indifference, wreathed in the mingled scents of wood polish and aged Scotch.

Instinctively, Jack peeled off his sunglasses and recorded the bar's layout, but the details sifted right through his conscious mind to be stored away for future reference. His main focus, his only focus, was the woman who swiveled at the sound of his foot-steps.

His first thought was that she hadn't changed. Her mink brown hair still tumbled in a loose ponytail down her back. Her cinnamon eyes still looked out at the world through a screen of thick, black lashes. In her short-sleeved red top and trim-fitting tan shorts, she looked more like a teenager on vacation than a respected historian with a long string of initials after her name.

Not until he stepped closer did he notice the differences. The Ellie he'd known nine years ago had glowed with youth and laughter and a vibrant joy of life. This woman showed fine lines of stress at the corners of her mouth. Shadows darkened her eyes, and he saw in their brown depths a wariness that echoed his.

She didn't smile. Didn't ease her stiff-backed pose. Silence stretched between them. She broke it, finally, with a cool greeting.

"Hello, Jack."

He'd expected to feel remnants of the old anger, the resentment, the fierce hurt. He hadn't expected the punch to his gut that came with the sound of her voice. His head dipped in a curt nod. It was the best he could manage at the moment.

"Thanks for coming," she said cooly.

He moved closer, wanting her to see his face when he delivered the speech he'd been preparing since Lightning informed him of the nature of his mission.

"Let's get one thing straight, right here and right now. My job is to protect you. That's the reason I'm here. That's the *only* reason I'm here."

Her chin snapped up. The fire he remembered all too well flared hot and dark in her eyes.

"I didn't imagine you'd make the trip down to San Antonio for any other reason. We had our fun, Jack. We both enjoyed our little fling. But that's all it was. You made that quite clear when you walked away from me nine years ago."

His jaw tightened. He had no answer for that. There *was* no answer. Eyes hard, he watched her slide off the bar stool. Her scent came with her as she approached, a combination of sun and the delicate cactus pear perfume she'd always worn. It was her mother's concoction, he remembered her telling him. He also remembered that he'd been nuzzling her neck at the time. Deliberately, Jack slammed the door on the thought.

When she raised a hand to shove back a loose tendril of hair, however, the gleam of silver circling her wrist brought another, sharper memory. The two-inch-wide beaten silver bracelet had cost him a half-month's pay. He'd slipped it onto her wrist mere moments before her uncle's police had arrived to arrest him.

"Let's go upstairs," he instructed tersely. "I want to see the message your friend left you."

Chapter 2

Wrapping her arms around her middle, Ellie stood just inside the door of the trashed suite.

"I moved to another room. The hotel wanted to clean up the mess, but I asked them to leave it until you got here."

His face impassive, Jack surveyed the mess. "Did the police find anything?"

"They dusted for prints, interviewed the hotel staff and asked for a complete inventory of the missing items, but as far as I know, they haven't come up with any concrete leads. In fact..."

"In fact?"

Her shoulders lifted under the chili red top. "The detective in charge was somewhat less than sympathetic. Evidently he read the story about me in the *Light* and doesn't take kindly to Mexicans determined to rewrite Texas history. It doesn't seem to make a whole lot of difference to some folks that I'm as American as they are.''

"No, it wouldn't.''

Jack had seen more than his share of bigotry during his overseas tours, both in the Marines and as an OMEGA agent. It didn't matter what a person's race, creed or financial circumstances might be. There was always someone who hated him or her because of them. With a mental note to establish liaison with the detective handling Ellie's case as soon as he conducted his preliminary assessment of the situation, he eyed the message on the mirror.

The wording suggested a man, someone familiar with weapons and not afraid to let Ellie know it. The obvious inference was that the threat stemmed from her work. Jack never trusted the obvious.

"I want a complete background brief on the members on your team,'' he told her, making a final sweep of the premises. "Particularly anyone who might or might not have a grudge against the team's leader.''

Startled, she dropped her arms. "You think one of my own people is responsible for this?''

"I don't think anything at this point. I'm just assessing the situation.''

Her eyes huge, she stared at him. Jack could see

the doubt creep into their cinnamon brown depths, followed swiftly by dismay. Only now, he guessed, was it occurring to her that the leak to the press might have been more deliberate than accidental. That one of her team members might, in fact, be working behind the scenes on some hidden agenda of his or her own.

The years fell away. For a moment, he caught a glimpse in her stricken face of the trusting, passionate girl she'd once been.

He'd come so close to loving that girl. Closer than he'd ever come to loving anyone who didn't wear khaki. Until Ellie, the Marines had been his life. Until Ellie, the Corps had constituted the only family he'd ever wanted or needed. He'd never known his father's name. He'd long ago buried the memory of the mother who left her four-year-old son in the roach-infested hotel room and drove off with some poor slob she'd picked up in a bar. After years of being passed from one foster home to another, Jack had walked into a recruiting office on his eighteenth birthday, signed up and found a home.

He shot up through the ranks, from private to corporal to gunnery sergeant in minimal time. He learned to follow and to lead. Because of his outstanding record, he was selected for the elite Marine Security Guard Battalion. His first tour was at the U.S. Embassy in Gabon, Africa, his second at the plush post in Mexico City.

The debacle in Mexico City had ended his career and destroyed all sense of family with the Corps. Thankfully, he'd found another home in OMEGA. This one, he vowed savagely, he wouldn't jeopardize by tumbling Ellie into the nearest bed.

"I also want a copy of your list of missing items."

The dismay left Ellie's face. Stiffening at his curt tone, she gave him an equally succinct response. "I'll print you out a copy. It runs to more than fifty pages."

"Fifty pages!"

The exclamation earned him a condescending smile. "My team's been on-site for almost a week now. We've recorded hundreds of digital images, cross-indexed them and made copious notes concerning each. The data was all stored in the external FireWire drive that was stolen. Thank God I backed the files up via the university's remote access mainframe!"

With that heartfelt mutter, she led the way down the hall to the new set of rooms the hotel had assigned her. Jack followed, forcing himself to keep his gaze on her back, her hair, the stiff set to her shoulders under her top. On anything, dammit, but the seductive sway of her hips.

A swift prowl around the spacious corner suite she showed him to had him shaking his head. "Pack your things."

"I beg your pardon?"

"I'll call the front desk and get them to move us."

"Why?"

He dragged back the gauzy curtains covering the corner windows. One set of wavy glass panes fronted the street. The other set faced the brick wall of the River Center complex next door.

"See the roof of that building?"

"Yes."

"It's on a direct line with these windows. Anyone with a mind to it could get a clear bead on a target in this room. Or climb up on the roof of that IMAX theater across the street and stake you out."

The color leached from her cheeks. "If you're trying to scare me, you're doing one heck of a good job."

"You should be scared. That wasn't a valentine your visitor left on that mirror, you know."

"Of course I know! To paraphrase your earlier remark, the viciousness of that threat is the reason, the *only* reason, I agreed to the nuisance of a bodyguard."

Hooking his thumbs in his jeans pockets, Jack tried to get a handle on the woman who'd emerged from the girl he'd once known.

"So why are you hanging around San Antonio, Ellie? Why offer yourself as a target to the kook or malcontent who issued that warning?"

"Because I refuse to let said kook or malcontent interfere with my work. In all modesty, I'm good at what I do. Damned good.'' She speared him with a hard look. ''You predicted I would be. Remember, Jack? Right about the time you and Uncle Eduardo jointly decided finishing college was more important to me than my... Let's see, how did he phrase it? My passing infatuation with a hardheaded Marine.''

They'd have to scratch at the old scars sometime. Better to do it now and give the scabs time to heal again. If Jack was to protect her, he needed her trust. Or at least her cooperation. He wouldn't gain either until he'd acknowledged his culpability for the hurt she'd suffered all those years ago.

''You were only nineteen, Ellie. I thought... Your uncle thought...''

''That I didn't know my own mind.'' Her chin came up. ''You were wrong. I knew it then. I know it now.''

She couldn't have made her meaning plainer. Jack Carstairs wouldn't get the chance to wound her again. He accepted that stark truth with a nod.

''Why don't we get settled in different rooms, and you can tell me exactly what it is you're so good at. I need to understand what you're doing here,'' he said to forestall the stiff response he saw coming, ''and why it's roused such controversy.''

The hotel staff moved them to adjoining suites two floors down. The rooms looked out over the inner courtyard of the hotel instead of the street. Like the rest of the historic hotel, they were furnished with a combination of period antiques and modern comfort. A burned-wood armoire held a twenty-seven-inch TV and a well-stocked bar. The wrought-iron bedstead boasted a queen-size mattress and thick, puffy goose-down comforter.

While Jack checked phones, door locks and ceiling vents, three valets transferred boxes of files and equipment on rolling dollies. Ruthlessly rearranging the furniture to meet her work-space needs, Ellie promptly turned her sitting room into a functional office. She'd already replaced the stolen computer and hard drive, which she now hooked up to an oversize flat LCD screen.

A smaller unit sat beside the computer. Jack studied it with a faint smile. Mackenzie Blair, OMEGA's chief of communications, would light up like a Christmas tree if she caught sight of all those buttons and dials and displays. The palm-size unit was probably crammed with more circuitry than the Space Shuttle.

Evidently Ellie Alazar shared Mackenzie's fascination with electronic gadgetry. She gave the small metal box the kind of pat a fond mother might give a child.

"This holds the guts of a technology I developed the summer after we…" Her brown brows slashed down. Obviously impatient with her hesitation, she plowed ahead. "The summer after I met you. I didn't make the trip to Mexico City that year. I didn't go down for several years, as a matter of fact.''

Jack wasn't surprised. Elena's emotions ran close to the surface. In the short months he'd known her, she'd never once reined them in. Looking back, he could see that was what had drawn him to her in the first place. Everything she thought or felt was all there, in her eyes, her face. Impatience, passion, anger—whatever emotion gripped her, she shared. Honestly. Openly.

She'd certainly shared her feelings the day her uncle sent his police to arrest Jack. She'd been furious with Eduardo Alazar. But not half as angry as she'd became with the Marine who refused to stand and fight for her.

''You didn't go to Mexico that summer,'' Jack acknowledged, steering the conversation to less volatile subjects. ''What did you do?''

''I worked for the National Park Service on a dig in the Pecos National Park. We were excavating the site of the battle of Glorietta Pass. The battle took place in 1862 and was one of the pivotal engagements in the Civil War.''

''The Gettysburg of the West. I've heard of it.''

She gave him a look of approval. ''Then you know the battle turned the tide against Confederates and sent Silbey's Brigade scuttling back to Texas in total disarray.''

Another Texas defeat. Evidently Ellie had started

her career at the site of one disastrous conflict for the Lone Star state. Now she was up to her trim, tight buns in controversy over another. No wonder some loyal local citizens wanted to roll up the welcome mat and send her on her way.

"We used metal detectors to locate shell casings at the battle site," she explained, warming to her subject. "We marked their location on a computerized grid, then categorized the casings by make and caliber. We also analyzed the rifling marks on the brass to determine the type of weapon that fired them."

"Sounds like a lot of work."

"It was. Three summers' worth of digging and mapping. Plus hundreds of hours of detailed research into the weaponry of the time. The Confederates tended to carry a wide variety of personally owned rifles and side arms. Union weapons were somewhat more standardized. By matching spent shell casings to the type of weapon that fired them, we were able to map the precise movement of both armies on the battlefield. We also built a massive database. For my Ph.D. dissertation, I expanded and translated the raw data into a program that allows forensic historians to reliably identify shell casings from any era post-1820."

"Why 1820?"

"The copper percussion cap was invented in the 1820s. Within a decade, two at most, almost every army in the world had converted its muzzle-loading flintlocks to percussion. More to the point where my research was concerned, the copper casing retained more defined rifling marks, which aided in identification of the type of weapon that fired it.''

Jack was impressed. He could fieldstrip an M-15, clean the components and put it back together blindfolded. He'd qualified at the expert level on every weapon in the Marine Corps inventory, as well as on the ones OMEGA outfitted him with. Yet his knowledge of the science of ballistics didn't begin to compare with Ellie's.

''So how do we get from the invention of the percussion cap to your finding that the hero of the Alamo deserted his troops and ran away?''

''It's not a finding.'' She shot the answer back. ''It's only one of several hypotheses I surfaced for discussion with my team. Honestly, you'd think simple intellectual curiosity would make folks wait to see whether the theory is substantiated by fact before they get all in a twit.''

''You'd think,'' Jack echoed solemnly.

Flushing a bit, she backpedaled. ''Sorry. I didn't mean to snap. I'm just getting tired of having to deal with outraged letters to the editor, picketers at the site, skittish team members and a nervous National Park Service director who's close to pulling the plug on our funding.''

There they were again. The fire, the impatience.

She hadn't learned to bank, either. Jack found himself hoping she never did.

"And this hypothesis is based on what?" he asked, the evenness of his tone a contrast to hers. "Start at the beginning. Talk me through the sequence of events."

"It would be better if I showed you." She speared a glance at her watch. "It's only a little past two. If you want, we can start here at the Alamo, then drive out to the site."

"Good enough. Give me ten minutes."

With the controlled, smooth grace that had always characterized him, he executed what Ellie could only describe as an about-face and passed through the connecting door. It closed behind him, leaving her staring at the panels.

The old cliché was true, she thought with a little ache. You can take a man out of the Marines, but you never quite took the Marine out of the man.

Like dust blown by the hot Texas wind, memories skittered through her mind. She could see Jack the night they'd met. She'd accompanied her aunt and uncle to a formal function at the American embassy. As head of the security detail, Gunnery Sergeant Carstairs had stood just behind the ambassador, square-shouldered, proud, confident. And so damned handsome in his dress blues that Elena hadn't been able to take her eyes off him all evening.

She'd been the one to ask him to dance. *She'd*

called him a few days later, inviting him to join her for a Sunday afternoon stroll through Chapultapec Park. *She'd* let him know in every way a woman could that she was attracted to him.

And that's all it was. A sizzling, searing attraction. At first.

How could she know she'd fall desperately in love with the man? That she'd find a passion in Jack's arms she'd never come close to tasting before? That she'd swear to give up everything for him—her scholarship, her family, her pride—only to have him throw them all back in her face.

If she closed her eyes, she could replay their final scene in painful, brilliant color. Jack was already under house arrest. Her uncle's overly protective, knee-jerk reaction to his niece's affair had forced the U.S. ambassador to demand Sergeant Carstairs's immediate reassignment and possible disciplinary action.

Steaming, Ellie had ignored her uncle's stern orders to the contrary, marched to the marine barracks and demanded to see Jack. He'd come to the foyer, stiff and remote in his khaki shirt and blue trousers with the crimson stripe down each leg. With brutal honesty, he'd laid his feelings on the line.

Ellie still had a year of college and at least three years of grad school ahead of her. He was going home to face a possible court-martial and an uncertain future. He refused to make promises he might not be able to keep. Nor would he allow her put her future on hold for his.

He was so noble, Ellie had railed. So damned, stupidly obstinate. Traits he continued to demonstrate even after they both returned to the States.

Cringing inside, Ellie recalled the repeated attempts she'd made to contact Jack. He wouldn't return her calls. Never answered her letters. Finally, her pride kicked in and she left a scathing message saying that he could damned well make the next move. He never did.

Now here they were, she thought, blowing out a long breath. Two completely different people. She'd fulfilled the early promise of a brilliant career in history. Jack, apparently, had bottomed out. Despite his extensive training and experience in personal security, he'd evidently drifted from one firm to another until going to work for some small-time operation in Virginia. Ellie wouldn't have known he was in the bodyguard business if one of her colleagues hadn't stumbled across his company on the Internet while preparing for a trip to Bogotá, Colombia, the kidnap capital of the universe.

It was guilt, only guilt, that had made her insist on Jack when her uncle urged her to accept the services of a bodyguard. She'd caused the ruin of his chosen career. Her own had exceeded all expectations. The least she could do was throw a little business his way.

From the looks of him, he could use it. She didn't know what was considered the appropriate uniform for bodyguards, but her uncle's security detail had always worn suits and ties and walked around talking into their wristwatches. She couldn't remember seeing any of them in thigh-hugging jeans or wrinkled, blue-cotton shirts with the sleeves rolled up. Or, she thought with a small ache just under her ribs, black leather boots showing faint scuff marks.

More than anything else, those scratches brought home the vast difference between the spit-and-polish sergeant she'd once loved and the man in the other room. Her throat tight, Ellie turned to gather her purse and keys.

Jack flipped open the palm-size 'phone and punched a single key. One short beep indicated instant connection to OMEGA's control center.

"Control, this is Renegade."

OMEGA's chief of communications responded with a cheerful, "Go ahead, Renegade."

As little as a year ago, operatives at the headquarters stood by twenty-four hours a day to act as controllers for agents in the field. Mackenzie Blair's improvements in field communications allowed for instant contact with headquarters and eliminated the need for controllers. Instead, Mackenzie and her communications techs monitored operations around the clock.

Mostly Mackenzie, Jack amended. The woman spent almost all her waking hours at OMEGA. She needed a life. Like Jack himself, he thought wryly.

"I've made contact with the subject."

The terse report no doubt raised Mackenzie's brows. After all, the background dossier she'd compiled had included a summation of Elena Maria Alazar's affair with Sergeant Jack Carstairs.

"Tell Lightning I'm working the preliminary threat assessment. I'll report back when I have a better feel for the situation."

"Roger that, Renegade."

After signing off, Jack slid the small, flat phone into his shirt pocket and hiked his foot up on a handy footstool. His movements were sure and smooth as he drew a blue steel short-barreled automatic from its ankle holster. He made sure the safety was on, released the magazine, checked the load and pushed the magazine back in place. A tug on the slide chambered a round. With the 9 mm tucked in its leather nest, he shook his pant leg over his boot and rapped on the door to Ellie's room.

"Ready?"

Pulling on a ball cap in the same chili-pepper red as her top, she hooked a bag over her shoulder.

"Yes."

Chapter 3

Outside, the July sun blazed down with cheerful brutality. Exiting the hotel, Ellie turned right toward Alamo Plaza. Jack walked beside her, his eyes narrowed against the glare as he scanned the crowd.

It included the usual assortment of vendors and tourists, with a heavy sprinkling of men and women in Air Force blue. They were basic trainees, released for a few precious hours from the nearby Lackland Air Force Base. With their buzz-cut hair and slick sleeves, they looked so young, so proud of their uniform. So unprepared for the crises that world events could plunge them into at any moment.

What they didn't look like were riled-up patriots seeking vengeance on a historian who dared to question the courage of a local legend. Nonetheless, Jack didn't relax his vigilance.

"What do you know about the Alamo?" Ellie asked as they approached the mission.

"Not much more than what I absorbed from the John Wayne movie of the same name."

And in the data Mackenzie had pulled off the computers. Jack kept silent about the background file. Right now, he was more interested in Ellie's version of the Alamo's history.

"It's one of a string of five missions located along the San Antonio River, founded in the early 1700s," she informed him. "Originally designated Mission Antonio de Valero, it didn't become known as the Alamo until much later."

With a sweep of her arm, she gestured to the adobe structure dominating the wide plaza ahead.

"There it is. The shrine of Texas liberty."

The distinctive building stirred an unexpected dart of pride in Jack. As a symbol of independence, its image had been seared into his consciousness. Of course, all those John Wayne movies might have had something to do with the sensation.

"Originally the mission compound sat by itself, well across the river from the settlement of San Antonio de Bexar," Ellie related. "Now, of course, the city's grown up all around it."

They wove a path through sightseers snapping photo after photo. A red-faced, grossly overweight candidate for a stroke backed up to frame a shot, banging into several fellow tourists in the process. Swiftly, Jack took Ellie's elbow to steer her around the obstacle.

Just as swiftly, he released her.

Well, hell! Here it was, going on nine years since he'd last touched this woman. Yet one glide of his fingers along her smooth, warm skin set off a chain reaction that started in his arm and ended about six inches below his belt.

For the first time since Lightning's call some hours ago, Jack conceded maybe Eduardo Alazar had reason to be concerned. The fires weren't out. Not entirely.

Jack had been so certain the embarrassment he'd caused Ellie and himself had doused any residual sparks. The sudden flare of heat in his gut screamed otherwise. Clenching his jaw against the unwelcome sensation, he tried to concentrate on Ellie's recitation.

"A series of droughts and epidemics decimated the mission's religious population," she related. "In 1793 the structure was turned over to civil authorities. At that point, Spanish cavalry from Alamo de Parras in Mexico took occupancy, and the fort became known at the Pueblo del Alamo. When the Spanish were driven out of Mexico, Mexican troops moved in. About the same time, the Mexican gov-

ernment opened the province of Texas to foreign settlers.''

"Foreign meaning Americans?''

"Americans and anyone else who would put down
roots and, hopefully, help stem attacks on settlements
by the Commanches and Apaches. Given the proximity to the States, though, it's only natural that most
immigrants were Americans. Led by Stephen Austin,
they flooded in and soon outnumbered the Mexican
population five to one. It was only a matter of time
until they decided they wanted out from under Mexican rule.''

"Those pesky Texans,'' Jack drawled.

"Actually,'' she replied with a smile, "they called
themselves Texians then. Or Tejanos. But they *were*
pretty pesky. Tensions escalated, particularly after
General Antonio Lopez de Santa Anna seized control
of the Mexican government and abrogated the constitution. In the process, he also abrogated most of
the rights of the troublesome immigrants. There were
uprisings all over Mexico—and outright rebellion
here in Texas.

"After several small skirmishes, the Americans
declared their independence and sent a small force to
seize the Alamo. When Santa Anna vowed to march
his entire army north and crush the rebellion, the tiny
garrison sent out a plea for reinforcements. William
Travis, Jim Bowie and Davy Crockett, among others,
answered the call.''

The names sounded like a roll call of America's heroes. Jim Bowie, the reckless adventurer as quick with his wit as with his knife. Davy Crockett, legendary marksman and two-term member of Congress from Tennessee. William Barrett Travis, commander of the Texas militia who drew a line in the sand with his saber and asked every Alamo defender willing to stand to the end to cross it. Supposedly, all but one did so.

Those who did met the fate Ellie related in a historian's dispassionate voice.

"When Santa Anna retook the Alamo in March, 1836, he executed every defender still alive and burned their bodies in mass funeral pyres. Or so the few non-combatants who survived reported."

"But you think those reports are wrong."

"I think there's a possibility they *may* be."

With that cautious reply, she led the way through the small door set in the massive wooden gates fronting the mission. Inside, thick adobe walls provided welcome relief from the heat. A smiling docent stepped forward to greet them.

"Welcome to the Alamo. This brochure will give you... Oh!" The smile fell right off her face. "It's you, Dr. Alazar."

"Yes, I'm back again."

"Our museum director said you'd finished your research here."

"I have. I'm playing tourist this afternoon and showing my, er, friend around."

The docent's glance darted from Ellie to Jack and back again. Suspicion carved a deep line between her brows. "Are you planning to take more digital photos?"

"No. I've taken all I need."

"We heard those were stolen."

"They were," Ellie replied coolly. "Fortunately, I make it a practice to back up my work."

The volunteer fanned her brochures with a snap. "Yes, well, I'll let Dr. Smith know you're here."

"You've certainly made yourself popular around here," Jack commented dryly.

"Tell me about it! The exhibits are this way."

Exiting the church, they entered a long low building that had once served as the barracks and now housed a museum of Texas history. Ellie let Jack set the pace and read those exhibits that caught his interest.

They painted a chillingly realistic picture of the thirteen-day siege. There was Santa Anna's army of more than twelve hundred. The pitiful inadequacy of the defending force, numbering just over a hundred. Travis's repeated requests for reinforcements. The arrival of the Tennesseeans. The wild, last-minute dash by thirty-two volunteers from Goliad, Texas, through enemy lines. The final assault some hours before dawn on March sixth. The massacre of all defenders.

The mass funeral pyres that consumed both Texan and Mexican dead. The pitiful handful of non-combatants who survived.

The original of Travis's most famous appeal for assistance was preserved behind glass. Written the day after the Mexican army arrived in San Antonio, the letter still had the power to stir emotions.

Commander of the Alamo
Bexar, Fby 24th, 1836
To the People of Texas and All Americans in the World
Fellow Citizens & Compatriots
I am besieged by a thousand or more of the Mexicans under Santa Anna. I have sustained a continual bombardment & have not lost a man. The enemy has demanded a surrender at discretion, otherwise the garrison are to be put to the sword if the fort is taken. I have answered the demand with a cannon shot, and our flag still waves proudly on the walls. I shall never surrender nor retreat.
Then, I call on you in the name of Liberty, of patriotism, & of everything dear to the American character, to come to our aid with all dispatch. The enemy is receiving reinforcements daily & will no doubt increase to three or four thousand in four or five days. If this call is neglected, I am determined to sustain myself as

long as possible and die like a soldier who never forgets what is due to his own honor & that of his country.

Victory or death

William Barrett Travis

Lt. Col. Comdt

P.S. The Lord is on our side. When the enemy appeared in sight, we had not three bushels of corn. We have since found in deserted houses 80 or 90 bushels & got into the walls 20 or 30 head of Beeves.

Travis.

"Whew!" Jack blew out a long breath. "No wonder the mere suggestion that this man didn't die at the Alamo has riled so many folks. He certainly made his intentions plain enough."

Nodding, Ellie trailed after him as he examined the exhibits and artifacts reported to belong to the defenders, among them sewing kits, tobacco pouches and handwoven horsehair bridles and lariats. A small, tattered Bible tugged at her heart. It was inscribed to one Josiah Kennett, whose miniature showed an unsmiling young man in the wide-brimmed sombrero favored by cowboys and vaqueros of the time. Silver conchos decorated the hatband, underscoring how closely Mexican and Tejano cultures had blended in the days before war wrenched them apart.

When Jack and Ellie emerged into a tree-shaded courtyard, the serene quiet gave no echo of the cannons that had once thundered from the surrounding walls. Tourists wandered past quietly, almost reverently.

"Okay," Jack said, summarizing what he'd read inside. "Susanna Dickinson, wife of the fort's artillery officer, said that Travis died on the north battery. Travis's slave Joe said he saw the colonel go down after grappling with troops coming over the wall. They make a pretty convincing argument that William B. stuck to his word and died right here at the Alamo."

"An argument I might buy," Ellie agreed, "except that Susanna Dickinson hid in the chapel during the assault. After the battle, she reportedly saw the bodies of Crockett and Bowie, but never specifically indicated she saw Travis's. She probably heard that he died on the ramparts from other sources."

"What about Joe's report?"

"Joe saw his master go down during the assault, then he, too, hid. Travis could have been wounded yet somehow survived. The only document that indicates his body was recovered and burned with the others is a translation of a report by Francisco Ruiz, San Antonio's mayor at the time. Unfortunately, the translation appeared in 1860, years after the battle. The original has never been found, so there's no way to verify its authenticity."

She knew her stuff. There was no arguing that.

"On the other hand," she continued, "rumors that some of the defenders escaped the massacre ran rampant for years. One held that Mexican forces captured Crockett some miles away and hauled him before Santa Anna, who had him summarily shot. There's also a diary kept by a corporal in the Mexican army who claims he led a patrol sent out to hunt down fleeing Tejanos."

Her eyes locked with Jack's.

"Supposedly, his patrol fired at an escapee approximately five miles south of here, not far from Mission San Jose. The corporal was sure they hit the man, but they lost him in the dense underbrush along the river."

"Let me guess. That's the site you're now excavating."

"Right."

It could have happened, Jack mused. He'd experienced the confusion and chaos of battle. He knew how garbled reports could become, how often even the most reliable intelligence proved wrong.

Still, as they moved toward the building that housed a special exhibit of weaponry used at the Alamo, he found himself hoping the theory didn't hold water. A part of him wanted to believe the legend—that William Barrett Travis *had* drawn that line in the sand, then heroically fought to the death alongside Davy Crockett, Jim Bowie and the others. Texas deserved its heroes.

The museum director evidently agreed. Short, rotund, his wire-rimmed glasses fogging in the steamy heat, he stood in front of the door to the exhibit with legs spread and arms folded and greeted Ellie with a curt nod. "Dr. Alazar."

"Dr. Smith."

"Were you wishing access to those artifacts not on public display?"

"Yes, there's one rifle in particular I want to show my, er, associate."

Jack flicked her an amused glance. Obviously, Ellie wasn't ready to admit she'd been intimidated into acquiescing to a bodyguard.

"I'm sorry," the director replied with patent insincerity. "I must insist that you put all such requests in writing from now on."

Ellie's eyes flashed. Evidently Smith had just drawn his own line in the sand.

"I'll do that," she snapped. "I'll also apprise my colleagues in this and future endeavors of your generous spirit of cooperation."

She left him standing guard at his post. Jack followed, shaking his head. Elena Maria Alazar might be one of the foremost experts in her field, but she wouldn't win a whole lot of prizes for tact or diplomacy.

"Damn Smith, anyway," she muttered, still fuming. "I suspect he's the one who raised such a stink with the media. He seems to think I'm attacking him personally by questioning his research."

It sounded to Jack as though the man might have a point there. Wisely, he kept silent and made a mental note to have Mackenzie run a background check on the museum director.

"I'll show you the images of that shotgun later," Ellie said as they retraced their steps.

"Why is that particular weapon so significant?"

"It's a double-barreled shotgun, reportedly recovered after the battle. Records indicate William Travis owned just such a weapon, or one similar to it. It's almost identical to the one we recovered at the dig."

Tugging her ball cap lower on her brow to shield her eyes against the blazing sun, she wove a path through the milling crowd outside the Alamo and made for the elaborate, wrought-iron façade of the Menger.

"I wish I could convince Smith that I'm still wide open to all possible theories. And that I have no intention of caving in to threats, obscene phone calls or petty nuisances like putting my requests for access to historical artifacts in writing."

Her mouth set, she rummaged around in her shoulder bag, dug out a parking receipt and approached the parking valet.

"Why don't I drive?" Jack said easily, passing the

attendant his receipt instead. "I want to get the lay of the land."

He also wanted to make sure someone skilled in defensive driving techniques was at the wheel whenever Ellie traveled.

She didn't argue. When the Cherokee came down the ramp, its tires screeching at the tight turns, she tossed her bag into the back and slid into passenger seat. The ball cap came off. With a grateful sigh for the chilled air blasting out of the vents, she swiped the damp tendrils off her forehead.

"Which way?" Jack asked.

"Take a left, go past the Alamo Dome, then follow the signs for Mission Trail."

Propping her neck against the headrest, Ellie stared straight ahead. For the second time in as many hours, Jack sensed the accumulated stress that kept the woman beside him coiled as tight as a cobra.

"Tell me about these obscene phone calls. How many have you received?"

"Five or six." Her nose wrinkled. "They were short and crude. Mostly suggestions on where I could stick my theories. One of the callers was female, by the way, which surprised the heck out of me."

Nothing surprised Jack any more. "Did the police run traces?"

"They tried. But the calls came through the hotel switchboard, and there's something about the routing system that precluded a trace."

Jack would fix that as soon as they returned. The electronic bag of tricks Mackenzie had assembled for this mission included a highly sophisticated and not exactly legal device that glommed onto a digital signal and wouldn't let go.

"See that sign?" Ellie pointed to a historical marker in the shape of a Spanish mission. "This is where we pick up Mission Trail. You need to hang a left here."

"Got it."

Flicking on his directional signal, Jack turned left. A half mile later, he made a right. That was when he noticed the dusty black SUV. The Ford Expedition remained three cars back, never more, never less, making every turn Jack did. Frowning, he navigated the busy city streets for another few blocks before spinning the steering wheel. The Cherokee's tires squealed as he cut a sharp left across two lanes of oncoming traffic.

"Hey!" Ellie made a grab for the handle just above her window. "Did I miss a sign?"

"No."

He flicked a glance in the rearview mirror. The SUV waited until one oncoming vehicle whizzed passed, dodged a second and followed.

Ellie had figured out something was wrong. Craning her neck, she peered at the traffic behind them while Jack whipped around another corner. When the

SUV followed some moments later, he dug his cell phone out of his pocket and punched a single button.

"Control, this is Renegade."

"Renegade?"

Ignoring Ellie's startled echo, Jack waited for a response. Mackenzie came on a moment later.

"Control here. Go ahead."

"I'm traveling west on…" He squinted at the street sign that whizzed by. "On Alameda Street in south San Antonio. There's a black Expedition following approximately fifty meters behind. I need you to put a satellite on him before I shake him."

"Roger, Renegade. I'll vector off your signal."

"Let me know when you've got the lock."

"Give me ten seconds."

Jack did a mental count and got down to three before Mackenzie came on the radio.

"Okay, I see you. I'm panning back… There he is. Black Expedition. Now I just have to sharpen the image a little…" A moment later, she gave a hum of satisfaction. "He's tagged. I'm feeding the license plate number into the computer as we speak. How long do you want me to maintain the satellite lock?"

"Follow him all the way home. And let me know as soon as you get an ID."

"Will do."

"Thanks, Mac."

"Anytime," OMEGA's communications chief answered breezily.

Jack snapped the transceiver shut and slipped it into his shirt pocket. A quick glance at Ellie showed her staring at him in astonishment.

"Your company has a satellite at their disposal?"

"Several. Hang tight, I'm going to lose this joker."

Jack could see the questions in her eyes but didn't have time for answers right now. The first rule in personal protective services was to remove the protectee from any potentially dangerous situation. He didn't know who was behind the wheel of the SUV or what his intentions were. He sure as hell wasn't about to find out with Ellie in the car.

Stomping down on the accelerator, he took the next intersection on two wheels. Ellie gulped and scrunched down in her seat. Jack shot a look in the rearview mirror and watched the larger, heavier Expedition lurch around the corner.

Two turns later, they'd left the main downtown area and had entered an industrial area crisscrossed by railroad tracks. Brick warehouses crowded either side of the street, their windows staring down like unseeing eyes. Once again, Jack put his boot to the floor. The Cherokee rocketed forward, flew over a set of tracks and sailed into an intersection just as a semi bearing the logo of Alamo City Fruits and Vegetables swung wide across the same crossing.

"Look out!"

Shrieking, Ellie braced both hands on the dash. Her boots slammed against the floorboards.

Jack spun the wheel right, then left and finessed the Cherokee past the truck with less than an inch or two to spare. Smiling in grim satisfaction, he hit the accelerator again.

The bulkier Expedition couldn't squeeze through. Behind him, they heard the squeal of brakes followed by the screech of metal scraping metal. Still smiling grimly, Jack made another turn. A few minutes later, he picked up Mission Trail again, but this time he headed into the city instead of out.

"We'd better put off our visit to the site until tomorrow," he told Ellie. "By then I should have a better idea of who or what we're dealing with."

"Fine by me," she replied, wiggling upright in her seat.

Actually, it was more than fine. After that wild ride, her nerves jumped like grasshoppers on hot asphalt, and her kidneys were signaling a pressing need to find the closest bathroom.

Jack, on the other hand, didn't look the least flustered. He gripped the steering wheel loosely, resting one arm on the console between the bucket seats, and divided his attention between the road ahead and the traffic behind. She couldn't see his eyes behind the mirrored sunglasses, but not so much as a bead of nervous sweat had popped out on his forehead.

"Do you do these kinds of high-speed races often in your line of work?" she asked.

"Often enough."

"And you've been in the same business since you left the Corps?"

"More or less."

"How do you handle the stress?"

He flashed her a grin that reminded her so much of the man she'd once known that Ellie gulped.

"I'll show you when we get back to the hotel."

Chapter 4

"**Y**oga?"

Ellie's disbelieving laughter rippled through the sun-washed hotel room.

"You do yoga?"

"According to my instructor," Jack intoned solemnly, "one doesn't 'do' yoga. One ascends to it."

"Uh-huh. And who is this instructor?" she asked, forming a mental image of a tanned, New Age Californian in flowing orange robes.

"One of the grunts in the first platoon I commanded."

"You're kidding!"

"Nope. Dirwood had progressed to the master level before joining the Corps."

She shook her head. "You know, of course, you're blowing my image of United States Marines all to hell."

"Funny," Jack murmured, "I thought I'd pretty much already done that."

He peeled off his sunglasses, tucked them in his shirt pocket and propped his hips against the sofa back. His blue eyes spent several moments studying Ellie's face before moving south.

She withstood his scrutiny calmly enough but knew she looked a mess. Sweat had painted damp patches on her scoop-necked top, and her khaki shorts boasted more wrinkles than Rip Van Winkle. She was also, as Jack proceeded to point out, a bundle of nerves.

"You're wound tighter than baling wire. You have been since I arrived."

No way was she going to admit that a good chunk of the tension wrapping her in steel cables stemmed as much from seeing him again after all these years as from the problems on the project.

"I've had a lot on my mind," she replied with magnificent understatement.

"It takes years to really master yoga techniques, but I could teach you a few of the basic chants and positions to help you relax."

Somehow Ellie suspected that getting down on the floor and sitting knee-to-knee with Jack would prove anything but relaxing. Part of her wanted to do it, if for no other reason than to test her ability to withstand the intimacy. Another part, more mature, more experienced—and more concerned with self-preservation—knew it was wiser to avoid temptation altogether.

"Maybe later," she said with a polite smile.

"It's your call."

"So what do we do now?"

"We wait until I get a report on the SUV."

Sitting twiddling her thumbs with Jack only a few feet away didn't do any more to soothe Ellie's jangled nerves than getting down on the floor with him would have.

"Since we've got the time now," she suggested, "why don't I show you some of the digital images I took at the Alamo and at the excavation site?"

"Good enough."

"I'll boot up the computer. Drag over another chair."

More than agreeable to the diversion, Jack hooked a chair and hauled it across the room. It was obvious why she'd shied away from his offer to teach her some basic relaxation techniques. She was jumpy as a cat around him. Not a good situation. For either of them.

A tense, nerve-racked client could prove too demanding and distracting to the agent charged with his or her protection. Jack's job would be a whole lot easier if he could get her to relax a little. Not enough to let down her guard. Not so much she grew careless. Just enough that the tension didn't leave her drained of energy or alertness.

Still, he had to admit to a certain degree of relief that she'd turned down his offer. The mere thought of folding Ellie's knees and elbows and tucking her into the first position was enough to put a kink in Jack's gut. Breathing in her potent combination of sun-warmed female and cactus pear perfume didn't exactly unkink it, either. Scowling, he focused his attention on the long list of files that appeared on the computer screen.

"We'll start at the Alamo," Ellie said, dragging the cursor down the list. "I want to show you the shotgun I was talking about."

"The one the museum director refused to let us see this afternoon?"

"Yes. I think the armament images pick up right about…" The cursor zipped down the indexed files. "Here."

Brilliant color flooded the seventeen-inch active matrix screen. There was Ellie in the Alamo's courtyard, smiling at the short, rotund director who gestured with almost obsequious delight to the entrance of the building housing his prized arms exhibit. Tourists crowded the courtyard around and behind them.

One mugged at an unseen camera. Another waited with an expression of impatience for Ellie and Smith to move out of the way. But the shot of Smith's face was clear and unobstructed.

"I'd like to send a copy of this image to a security analyst," Jack said. "Can you flag it for later reference?"

"Yes, of course. But…" Looking uncomfortable, Ellie turned to face him. "Smith is just trying to protect his turf. I don't like the idea of invading his privacy or compiling a secret file on him. Or on any of my colleagues, for that matter."

"We won't be compiling secret files," he answered mildly. "Merely exploiting those that already exist. You'd be amazed at how much data is floating around out there about John Q. Public."

"Yes, but…"

"Flag the image, Ellie."

With obvious reluctance, she went to the menu at the top of the screen and bookmarked the file.

Jack leaned forward, peering intently at the images that flashed by after that. More shots in the courtyard. The interior of the museum, with room after room of weaponry of the type used during the siege of the Alamo. The special exhibits, not open to the public.

"For the most part," Ellie explained, "these are pieces that have yet to be authenticated. They were either excavated in or around the Alamo or donated by descendants of the combatants.''

A click of the mouse brought up a vividly detailed image of a long-barreled rifle.

''This is a Brown Bess, so known because the troopers allowed the steel barrel to burnish and thus prevent glare that could distort their aim. This smooth-bore musket served as the standard infantry rifle carried by the British during the Napoleonic Wars. After the war, the Brits sold their excess inventories to armies all over the world.''

''Including the Mexican army?''

''Yes, well, Mexico was still ruled by Spain then. When it won its independence, its army pretty well retained the standard-issue armaments. Historical documents indicate Santa Anna's infantry was armed with the Brown Bess. Most had been converted from muzzle-loading flintlock to percussion by then.''

She flashed up another image of the musket and highlighted the differences in the firing mechanism.

''By contrast,'' she continued, ''the Tejanos who fought at the Alamo carried weapons as diverse as the defenders themselves. They weren't members of a regular army, remember. They were settlers—farmers, ranchers, doctors, lawyers, ministers and slaves—all rebelling against Santa Anna's edicts dispossessing them of their rights under the former Constitution. They were also adventurers like Jim Bowie.

Patriots like Davy Crockett and his Tennesseeans. Slaves, like Bowie's man Joe. They came armed with everything from Spanish blunderbusses to French muskets to long-barreled Kentucky hunting rifles, fowlers and shotguns.''

She ran through a series of images, identifying each weapon as it came up. When the image of a particular shotgun filled the screen, her voice took on an unmistakable hint of excitement.

''We know from various accounts that Travis arrived at the Alamo armed with a double-barrel shotgun like this one. He'd written several letters to Stephen Austin, advocating the gun as the standard weapon for the newly organized Texas cavalry. It didn't have the range of long rifle, of course, but it provided lethal firepower at closer range.''

With a click of the mouse, she rotated the three-dimensional image.

''Note the stock. It's made of curly maple, sometimes called tiger tail or fiddleback.''

Another click zoomed in on the silver inlays on the side of the stock.

''See the gunsmith's mark on the butt plate? It traces to a gunsmith in Sparta, South Carolina.''

Close at her shoulder, Jack could feel her controlled excitement straining to break loose as she returned to the index, scrolled down several pages and clicked on another file.

An outdoor scene was painted across the screen. A narrow creek twisted through the background, its banks almost lost amid a dense tangle of cotton-woods. A small group stood at the edge of one bank. Ellie and her team, Jack guessed, scrutinizing each of their faces in turn.

"Flag this photo, too," he instructed.

Her lips thinned, but she bookmarked the file. That done, she zoomed in on one of the objects lying on a piece of canvas at the team's feet. It was a shotgun, similar to the one she'd brought up on the screen moments ago. But this barrel sported a thick coat of rust. The silver mountings had tarnished to black, and wood rot riddled the stock.

Ellie enlarged the image again. "Look at the butt plate on this one. The gunsmith's mark is hard to read, but it's there."

Jack leaned closer, squinting at the screen. "Looks like the same mark."

"It is. Did I mention the gunsmith lived in Sparta, South Carolina?"

"You did."

"And that William Barrett Travis grew up, went to school and opened his first law practice in Sparta?"

"No, You saved that bit for last." Grinning at her air of triumph, he played devil's advocate. "Okay. I'm a betting man. I'd say you could lay odds Travis carried a gun made for him by a smith in his hometown *into* the Alamo. But someone could have picked up the gun when Travis went down and carried it *out,* including any one of a thousand Mexican soldiers.''

''As a matter of fact, Deaf Smith, a scout for Houston, captured a Mexican courier a month later using saddlebags monogrammed W.B. Travis.''

She swiveled her chair sideways, her eyes alive with the enjoyment of an intellectual debate.

''Who's to say those saddlebags weren't taken off a horse found wandering beside a creek five miles south of the Alamo? We're, uh, hoping DNA testing will help…you know…confirm…''

She stuttered to a halt. They were close. Too close. Almost nose to nose. Jack could see the gold flecks in her eyes. Feel the warm wash of her breath on his skin. If he leaned forward an inch, just another inch…

Abruptly, he jerked back in his seat.

Ellie made the same move at precisely the same moment. Chagrin, dismay and a touch of irritation chased across her face. She opened her mouth, only to snap it shut again when the small device in Jack's shirt pocket gave off a high-pitched beep. He pulled out the phone, glanced at the digital display and swung to his feet.

''Renegade here. Go ahead, control.''

Mackenzie Blair came on the line. "I ran the Expedition's tag. It's registered to a Mr. Harold Berger, 2224 River Drive, Austin, Texas."

"What have you got on the man?"

"Nothing much, seeing as Mr. Berger died two years ago. His wife reports that he never owned an Expedition, black or otherwise."

Jack's glance went to Ellie, still seated in front of her computer. The tension that had jolted through him seconds ago returned, doubled in intensity.

"Interesting," he muttered.

"Isn't it?" Mackenzie replied. "I did a screen of credit cards issued to Mr. H. Berger at his Austin address. I found an American Express and a Visa card, issued six months after he died."

Jack paced the sitting room, the phone tight against his ear. "What about the Expedition's driver? Did you get a picture of whoever emerged from the vehicle after it hit the truck?"

"Negative. He didn't get out of the vehicle. Not at the scene, anyway. He backed up, peeled off and squealed into a five-story parking garage about a mile away. Unfortunately, our spy satellites can't look through five layers of concrete, so I didn't get a shot of him exiting the vehicle. I contacted the San Antonio police and asked them to check it out. They found it abandoned and wiped clean of prints."

"Figures."

"I thought you should know one of their gun-sniffing dogs alerted on it. They found traces of gun-powder residue in the front seat."

Jack wasn't liking the sound of this. A stolen identity. Gunpowder residue. No prints. His gut told him they weren't talking a short, balding museum director here. Or a highly credentialed member of a scientific team. They were talking a pro.

"I'm going to send you a batch of digital images," he told Mackenzie. "We'll put names to the folks we know. I want you to run complete background checks on them and screen the rest for anyone or anything that looks suspicious."

"No problem."

"When can I expect results?"

"I don't know. How many images are we talking about?"

"Hang on." He cut to Ellie. "How many digital files have you got stored on the computer?"

"About six hundred."

"How many of those do you estimate include images of people?"

Her forehead wrinkled in concentration. "Live persons, I'd guess about two hundred. If you include the skeletal remains, another hundred or so."

"We'll start with those folks who are still breathing," Jack drawled. "Get ready to send copies."

Her brows soared. "Of all two hundred?"

"All two hundred."

"Two hundred!" OMEGA's chief of communications gave a groan. "And here I actually planned to beat the traffic home tonight, order a pizza and sneak in a little tube time."

"Sorry, Mac. Have your pizza delivered to the Control center and charge it to me."

"Don't think I won't," she grumbled. "Okay, I'll stand by to receive. Tell Dr. Alazar to fire off those files when ready."

They started popping up on the Control Center's screens fifteen minutes later. Dr. Alazar had converted the images contained in each file to JPEG format, thank goodness. JPEG files took a little longer to load but produced clear, sharp pictures.

Mackenzie worked the easy ones first, those with flags indicating Dr. Alazar had identified the individuals in the photos. One by one, she fed the names into a program linked to financial, government, merchandising and criminal databases worldwide. Within moments, she'd know whether any of these scholarly looking individuals had ever been cited for jaywalking, rented porn movies or fudged on his income taxes.

"Anything I can help you with, chief?"

Dragging her eyes from the screen, Mackenzie

glanced at her subordinate. John Alexander had put in at least five more years at OMEGA than she had but cheerfully cited his wife and four kids as reason for remaining as a mid-level tech with semiregular hours instead of moving up to the chief's job when it had come open. With all his experience, John was a good man to have at headquarters and a wizard in the field when it came to planting bugs that absolutely defied detection.

"As a matter of fact," Mackenzie said with a grin, "I was just going to send the cavalry to search for you. Renegade sent us a tasking."

She got him started on the unflagged files. Since they didn't have IDs on the folks in those photos, John would have to scan the images one by one and run them through a program that captured each subject's skin, hair and eye color, estimated weight and height and any discernible scars, tattoos or disfigurements. The physical characteristics would then be fed into FBI, CIA and national crime information center computers for potential matches. Information extracted by this method wasn't as accurate as fingerprints, DNA sampling or retinal scans, but the matches ran something close to seventy percent. If nothing else, they provided a starting point.

"Geez," John muttered as he opened the first file. "There must be ten or twelve people in this shot.

They look like a bunch of tourists. Do you want me to scan all of them?''

"Let me see."

Mackenzie rose out of her seat and bent over the console to view his screen. That was how Lightning found her when he strolled into the control center a moment later, a pizza carton held shoulder-high and balanced on his fingertips.

He paused for a moment, unabashedly enjoying the view. Most days, Nick looked, acted and thought like an American, but he'd been born in Cannes and possessed a Frenchman's esteem for the finer points of the female form. And Mackenzie's round, trim rear certainly qualified as fine.

Unfortunately, the same rules that prohibited an agent from becoming involved with a subject during operations applied in triplicate to OMEGA's director and his chief of communications. As long as one of his agents was in the field, Lightning couldn't allow himself or anyone on his staff to become distracted. Still, his eyes glinted with masculine appreciation as he made his way across the control center.

"This was just delivered downstairs," he said casually. "I assume you ordered it."

Mackenzie scrambled off the console. "If it's a sausage, double pepperoni and jalapeño special, I did."

Nick's eyes closed in something close to real pain. Dear Lord. Sausage, double pepperoni and jalapeño.

"Have you ever tasted pizza the way they make it along the Riviera?"

"My last cruise in the Navy was to the Med," Mackenzie informed him, lifting the lid to sniff appreciatively. "We dropped anchor just off San Remo. As I recall, the northern Italians doused everything, including their pizzas, in white cream sauce. Yuck!"

"A good cream sauce can be one of life's most decadent pleasures," Nick replied with a lift of one brow. "You'll have to let me take you to one of my restaurants sometime so you can sample it done right."

And that would be, Mackenzie thought, right about the time she developed a severe death wish.

She didn't play in Nick Jensen's league and knew it. If her short, disastrous marriage had taught her nothing else, it was to avoid smooth, handsome charmers like this one at all costs. Now if only she could keep her nerves from crawling around under her skin when he came to stand beside her.

"What are you working?"

"A request from Renegade. He's forwarded a series of images and asked for IDs and background checks."

Nick's blond brows drew together. In the blink of

an eye, he transitioned from every woman's ultimate sex fantasy into OMEGA's cool, take-charge director.

"I don't like that business with the Expedition this afternoon. Give Renegade whatever he asked for and then some."

Whipping to attention, Mackenzie snapped him a salute. "Aye, aye, *sir!*"

He eyed her for a moment, his expression inscrutable. She held the exaggerated pose until he left the control center, then turned to her assistant with a wry grin.

"Guess that answers your question, John. Scan every warm body in those photos."

Chapter 5

Ellie's team returned to the hotel from the excavation site a little past six that evening. The first team member to rap on her door was a tall, rangy, twenty-something male with a shock of dark red hair. He looked surprised when Jack answered his knock. Even more surprised when Ellie introduced the newcomer as an old friend.

"Jack's in the security business," she explained. "He flew in this morning to help us deal with some of the nastiness we've been subject to recently. Jack, this is Eric Chapman. He's one of my graduate students at the University of New Mexico."

Chapman's handshake was casual enough, but Jack picked up on the subtle signals that only the male of the species would recognize. Unless he missed his guess, the kid had a bad case of the hots for his professor and didn't particularly like the idea of another man poaching on his territory.

"So are we having a team meeting tonight, Ellie?"

"Yes. Eight o'clock, here in my room. Pass the word along to the others, would you?"

"Sure. How about dinner? Want to go down on the river and grab a quick bite?" His glance drifted to Jack. "If you two don't have plans, that is."

"We do," Jack answered, preempting Ellie's response.

She threw him a cool look but didn't contradict him. "I'll see you at the meeting, Eric. Tell the team I'd like a complete report of the afternoon's activities."

"Right."

When the door closed behind him, Ellie returned to the sitting room and regarded Jack with a slight frown. "I think we better establish some ground rules here, the first being that you consult with me before making arbitrary decisions."

"Like where you'll have dinner and who you'll have it with?"

"Exactly."

"Were you really that eager to go back out in the heat and chow down with the kid?" he asked, suddenly, acutely curious.

The intensity of his need to know whether she reciprocated Chapman's interest both surprised and irritated Jack. Somehow, he'd just skidded right past professional into personal. Very personal. Why the hell should he care if Ellie was providing the kid with private instruction after hours? Unless their relationship impacted Jack's ability to protect her, it wasn't any of his business. Technically.

Ellie evidently shared that opinion. Her voice chilly, she set him straight.

"No, I'm not all that eager to go back out in the heat. I simply prefer that you not make decisions for me. Or undermine my authority with my team," she added pointedly.

"Then you'd better make up your mind how you want me to interact with them. As your bodyguard or as old friend."

The chill didn't leave her eyes. If anything, it deepened. Toying with the silver bracelet banding her wrist, she debated her response.

Jack understood her hesitation. He'd piled up enough experience as an embassy guard and as a freelancer after leaving the Corps to appreciate how much take-charge executives hated to admit their fear. Hated, too, the helplessness that came with becoming a walking target. People in Ellie's position were used to calling the shots, not dodging them.

"Why don't we just stick with the explanation I gave Eric?" she suggested after a moment. "You *are* an old friend. You're also an expert in the security business. You flew in to assess the seriousness of the threats against me and my team.''

''Fine. We'll go with that. Now, about dinner. Mind if we order room service? I want you to give me a complete rundown on your team members before they assemble.''

Mackenzie would provide in-depth background dossiers once she'd screened the files they'd sent earlier, but Jack wanted Ellie's take. She'd worked with these people. She knew their strengths and weaknesses.

Now that she'd had time to think about it, she might also have some insight into whether one of them had deliberately leaked her controversial preliminary hypothesis to the media.

She didn't.

Flatly rejecting the idea that that a member of her group might be trying to sabotage the project, she spent the next two hours alternately detailing their impressive credentials and passionately defending them.

She hadn't changed much in that regard, Jack thought when he left her to prepare for the meeting and went next door to grab a quick shower. She'd defended a certain hardheaded Marine just as fiercely to her uncle…until Jack killed her arguments and her passion by rejecting both.

He'd taken the right stand, he told himself as he leaned against the shower tiles and lifted his face to the stinging needles. The *only* stand he could have taken, given the circumstances. Ellie had been so young then, with her whole future ahead of her. Jack couldn't see any future beyond being sent home in disgrace to face a possible court-martial, with all its potential for publicity.

The paparazzi would have eaten it up. The niece of the president of Mexico. An American Marine with a father whose name was a question mark and a mother who could be turning tricks in Detroit for all Jack knew. He'd never cared enough to track her down.

Then there were those searing, stolen hours in Mexico City. If the sensation-hungry media had gotten wind of those, the shinola would have hit the fan for sure. Jack had been insane to give in to Ellie's urgings, crazy to think he could give her release while holding back his own. On fire with impatience and need, she'd taken matters into her own hand. Literally. Even now, Jack could remember how her hot, eager fingers had brushed his aside and tugged at his zipper.

The memory slammed into him, hitting like a fist to the gut. He stiffened, felt himself get hard. Painfully hard. Cursing, he reached out and gave the shower knob a savage twist. Ice cold pellets shot into his skin from his neck to his knees. Gritting his teeth, Jack ducked his head under the stream.

His skin still prickled when he rapped on the connecting door fifteen minutes later. So did his temper, but he disguised his edginess behind a bland expression as Ellie's team began to congregate.

There were three besides Chapman. Orin Weaver, a noted forensic anthropologist who, Ellie explained, frequently acted as consultant for local, state and national law enforcement agencies. Janet Dawes-Hamilton, an archeologist from Baylor University. Sam Pierce, a field archeologist on the staff of the National Park Service, which owned the land on which the remains were discovered.

All except Chapman possessed Ph.D.s and an impressive string of published credits. All, including Chapman, eyed Jack with varying degrees of wariness. Like Ellie, they seemed to think the addition of a security specialist to their little group added a disturbing note of authenticity to the ugliness swirling around them.

"Sorry I didn't make it back to the site this afternoon," she said once the team had made themselves comfortable. "We were on our way but got involved in a high-speed chase through the streets of San Antonio."

The dry announcement produced the expected reactions. Gray-whiskered Orin Weaver blinked. The red-haired Chapman demanded to know if she was serious.

"Who was chasing whom?" Dr. Dawes-Hamilton asked in a cool, clipped voice.

"Person or persons unknown were after us," Jack answered. "We don't know who or why. Yet."

Pierce frowned and leaned forward, his callused hands clasped loosely between his knees. The National Park Service staffer didn't come across as a man out to harass his colleague into abandoning a dig or a particular theory, but Jack wasn't going to cut him any more slack than the others.

"I'll have to notify my headquarters about this latest incident," he said to Ellie. "They're already concerned over the adverse publicity our project has generated. One more mishap or media frenzy and...well..."

"The director may decide to shut down the dig," she finished for him. "With funding for future projects up before Congress," she explained to Jack, "he's nervous about offending the powerful Texas Congressional delegation."

"Not to mention the equally powerful President, who just happens to hail from the Lone Star state," Pierce put in dryly.

Jack kept to himself the fact that it was the President who'd requested OMEGA send an agent to San Antonio with instructions to protect Dr. Alazar and defuse the situation, if at all possible. From what he'd observed in the past eight hours or so, it might not be de-fusable.

Which is what he reported to Lightning later that night.

It was late, well past midnight. The meeting had broken up a little past ten. Jack waited until he was sure Ellie had settled into bed before slipping out to make his rounds. By the time he'd tested the hotel's security systems and satisfied himself as to the night staff's alertness, he was ready to drop into the rack himself. First, though, he gave Lightning his initial take on the situation.

"It's not smelling right. I'll make contact with the San Antonio police tomorrow to see what they've turned up, but that business about the Expedition being wiped clean bothers me."

"Me, too."

"How's Mac coming on those IDs and background checks?"

"Last time I checked, her pizza had gone stone cold and she had some rather uncomplimentary things to say about you."

"I'll bet."

"Hopefully, she and her folks will complete the runs within twenty-four hours. I'll stay on her."

Jack cocked a brow at the odd note in Lightning's voice. He'd dodged bullets and side-stepped pit vipers with the man during one memorable mission but still couldn't quite read him. None of the OMEGA agents could. Jensen came across as smooth and sophisticated, yet no one who'd ever witnessed his skill with a knife would willingly go blade-to-blade with him.

After signing off, Jack set the phone on the nightstand beside his bed and unbuttoned his shirt. His thoughts drifted to the time Lightning had lived up to his name and saved Jack's life with one lethal throw. Jack had returned the favor some months later while helping take down a band of gunrunners. Grunting with satisfaction at the memory, he shucked his shirt and had just reached to unbuckle his ankle holster when he heard the crash of metal and shattering glass next door.

Ellie's cry came through the wall, sharp with distress. Jack hit the connecting door a half second later, swearing viciously when he found it locked on the other side. One brutal kick with his heel splintered the wood and sprang the lock, slamming the door against the wall.

He dived through. Hit the floor in a roll. Came up in a crouch, the blue steel automatic aimed squarely at the woman who shrieked and stumbled back a few steps.

''Jack! Good God!''

Her obvious astonishment eased his blood-pumping tension a fraction. Only a fraction. Heart hammering, Jack swung in a full circle. There was no one else in the room. Only then did he straighten and record two separate impressions.

The first was an overturned room service tray, spilling the dinner Ellie had hardly touched across the carpet.

The second was her sleep shirt.

At least, that's what Jack assumed it was. It looked like a man's white cotton T-shirt, cut off a good six inches above the skimpiest damned pair of bikini briefs he'd ever laid eyes on. If that bite-size bit of nylon and lace wasn't a thong, it was close enough to raise an instant sweat on his palms.

Which, he realized belatedly, still gripped the automatic.

Swinging the barrel away from Ellie's midsection, he thumbed the safety. His breath came fast and hard through his nostrils, and his voice was distinctly unfriendly when he demanded to know what the hell she was doing.

"I was hungry," she fired back, shaken but recovering fast. "I intended to finish the salad I didn't eat earlier and tipped over the tray. I'm sorry I woke you."

Her stiff apology didn't cut it.

"I'm not talking about the damned tray! Why did you lock the door?"

His snarl snapped her chin up. Lips thinning, she speared a glance at the shattered wood.

"I wasn't afraid you were going to pay me a late-night visit and jump my bones, if that's what you're thinking.''

He wasn't. Now that she'd planted the idea, though, he knew he'd have to pry it out of his head with a crowbar. Along with the all-too-vivid image of her bare belly and long, slender flanks.

''Evidently an unlocked door is one of those ground rules we didn't cover,'' she said stiffly. ''Maybe we'd better sit down and spell them all out.''

Yeah. Right. With Jack stripped down to the waist and her in a scrap of nylon and last.

Not hardly!

''We'll spell them out tomorrow. For tonight, leave the door propped shut. And for God's sake, don't trip over any more trays.''

''I'll do my best.''

The sarcasm didn't win her any points. Shooting an evil look across the room, Jack made sure the dead bolt on the door to her suite was set, checked the window locks once more and retreated. His side of the connecting door closed with a small thud. A few seconds later, the shattered door on her side hit with a bang.

He was up before dawn the next morning. Showered and shaved, he took perverse pleasure in rapping on the door just past seven.

Some moments later, Ellie yanked it open. She'd

pulled a short silk robe over her T-shirt, thank God.
Her hair spilled over her shoulders in a rumpled free
fall. Sleep added a hoarse note to her voice when she
croaked at him.

"What?"

"I'm going to make a quick visit to the San Antonio police department. Don't leave the hotel until
I get back."

Still groggy, Ellie grunted an assent.

Never a morning person, she felt about as fresh
and perky as last week's leftovers. Her eyelids
scraped like sandpaper. Her mouth had that cottony
fuzz that cried for Scope. The fact that Jack was wide
awake, showered and looking lean and tough in snug
jeans and a black knit shirt that stretched taut across
his shoulders only added to her disgruntlement.

As she closed the door behind Jack, though, she
would have traded mouthwash and toothpaste *and*
half her next month's salary for a cup of black coffee.
She considered calling room service to order a pot,
but the prospect of explaining the broken dishes and
shattered connecting door nixed that notion. Any
more damage to their historic hotel and the Mengers'
management would probably call in the sheriff to
escort her out of town.

Shaking her head, Ellie padded into the bathroom
and turned the shower to full blast. Steam soon
wreathed the room. After shedding her robe and un-

dies, Ellie stepped into the stall and waited for the hot jets to work their restorative magic.

By the time Jack returned, she was dressed in a fresh pair of khaki shorts, a tan tank and a sleeveless khaki vest that came equipped with a half dozen handy pockets. With her hair tucked under a ball cap and a thick slathering of insect repellent coating all exposed areas of skin, she once again felt ready to take on all comers.

Jack included.

Chapter 6

"The police don't have anything on the Expedition yet."

Ellie accepted Jack's terse report with a nod. After her less than positive experience with the detective investigating her ransacked hotel room and the threats scrawled across her mirror, she hadn't really expected much.

"Have you had breakfast?" she asked, trying to tamp down her impatience to get out to the site. She'd already lost almost a whole day of work. With the National Park Service director waffling over the funding for the project, she didn't want to lose any more.

"I downed a cup of coffee and a breakfast burrito

while I was waiting for Detective Harris to put in an appearance at the precinct,'' Jack replied. ''How about you?''

''I'll grab some coffee on our way through the lobby.''

''You need more than that.''

''That's all I ever have in the mornings.''

Draping her heavy canvas bag over her shoulder, Ellie waited for him to join her at the door. Jack went out first, armed the anti-intrusion devices he'd installed and followed her down the hall.

Thankfully, the hotel provided complimentary coffee for its guests. Downing the hazelnut blend in quick, grateful gulps from a cardboard cup, Ellie settled into the passenger seat of Jack's rented Cherokee. This time, the drive down Mission Trail proved uneventful. No dusty SUVs with darkened windows chasing after them. No high-speed twists and turns. Only Ellie and Jack, thigh-to-thigh in the close confines of the rental vehicle.

By the time they pulled into the parking lot of Mission San Jose, she felt the need to put some immediate distance between her and the hard, muscled contours of his body.

''We could drive around to the dig,'' she informed him, shouldering open her door, ''but I thought you might want to see the mission compound first. It'll give you a better sense of what the Alamo was like back at the time of the siege.''

Slinging her canvas field bag over one shoulder, Ellie led the way down a gravel path. As always, Mission San Jose's tranquil setting and superb restoration thrilled both the historian and the aesthete in her. San Jose had been the largest and most active of the Texas religious settlements and, in her considered opinion, richly deserved its title as the Queen of the Missions.

The church boasted a large cupola dome, an exquisitely ornamented façade and the beautiful but curiously misnamed Rose Window, with elaborate carvings not of flowers but pomegranates. A rectangular granary with an arched roof dominated the opposite side of the compound from the church. The walls surrounding both were twelve feet thick, a potent reminder that these missions served secular as well as religious purposes.

"San Jose was founded in seventeen twenty," Ellie told Jack, their boots crunching the gravel path in a synchronized beat. "Just a few years after the Alamo. Like the other Texas missions, its purpose was to convert the local population to Catholicism, extend Spanish civilization in the New World and buttress the northern frontiers. At one time, the mission housed a population of more than three hundred priests, soldiers and Coahuiltecan Indians."

Signs spaced at intervals on the path pointed to various points of interest, including the park headquarters and gift shop. Ellie steered Jack past the main structures toward a gate in the far wall.

"The Indians farmed the surrounding countryside, producing corn, beans, potatoes, sugar cane and cotton, among other crops. They also maintained large herds of cattle, sheep and goats. Naturally, a rich settlement like this made for an irresistible target for hostile raids. When the Apache or Comanche threatened, the residents would drive their livestock inside the compound and hunker down behind San Jose's massive walls. Reportedly, they were never breached."

"Unlike those at the Alamo," Jack commented.

"Also unlike the Alamo, San Jose is still an active Catholic parish. Masses are said in the church, and I'm told it's a popular spot for weddings. The diocese maintains the church, and the National Park Service is responsible for the other structures and the outlying grounds."

Once through the small gate, they faced a wide, grassy field banded on three sides by a split rail fence. A twisting line of cottonwoods defined the fourth. As Jack and Ellie crossed the field toward the tree-lined creek, grasshoppers buzzed in the early morning heat and leaped out of their way. About halfway across the grassy field Ellie pointed out a series of small squares dug in the earth. Staked strands of wire surrounded each square. Red tags dangled from the wire.

"We've been using metal detectors to scan this field. Each of those tags marks a spot where we found spent cartridge shells. Most of the shells have rifling marks which suggest they were fired from Brown Besses similar to those used by the Mexican army. We also found several we think were fired by the shotgun we excavated down by the creek. We won't know for sure until we run a full ballistics analysis."

She tried to keep her voice properly dispassionate, but the thrill of discovery added a vibrancy she couldn't quite disguise. "Notice how those digs run in almost a straight line from north to south?"

Jack took a quick fix on the sun and nodded. Carefully, Ellie emphasized her point.

"The trail of expended bullets extends from the far corner of the Mission San Jose Park almost to the creek."

"By extrapolation," he said slowly, picking up on her lead, "from the Alamo to this spot five miles south, where a desperate defender might have raced for the tangle of trees to escape his pursuers, firing as he rode."

She beamed at him. "Exactly!"

His instant grasp of the significance of those small digs didn't surprise her. Jack Carstairs was no dummy. Except, she amended, when it came to his long-ago relationship with a passionate nineteen-year-old.

"The bullets track right to the spot where the skeletal remains were found," she related.

"Who found them?"

"The bullets or the bones?"

"The bones."

"A couple of boys. They snuck out of Sunday Mass and slipped away to play by the creek. When they spotted the bones, they ran yelling for their mom."

"Probably had nightmares for a month after that."

"I don't think so," Ellie replied, laughing. "I saw the news cam videotapes taken right after the find. The boys mugged like mad for the cameras. They seemed to think they'd landed right in the middle of a grand adventure. Even more so after the police and ME determined from the artifacts found with the bones that the find had historical significance."

"Is that when you were called in?"

"Yep. Because I'd done so much work for and with the National Park Service, the director contacted me and asked me to head up the team. He hasn't said so," she added with a wry grin, "but I'm pretty sure he's regretting his choice."

They were almost to the creek when Eric Chapman stepped out of the shadows and into the blazing sunlight. A metal detector extended from his left arm like a long, mechanical claw. When he spotted Ellie, a look of profound relief crossed his face.

"Hey, boss lady. You got here just in time."

"Uh-oh. What's up?"

"Another TV reporter, with cameraman in tow. Sam's trying his best to fob her off with the press release we hammered out last night, but she wants down and dirty details."

Ellie threw a glance at the trees. Just what she needed to start her day. A camera crew and more adverse publicity. Swallowing a sigh, she eyed the detector strapped to Eric's arm.

"We've pretty well covered this open field. Work the grids closer in to the mission today."

"Will do."

Jack's knowledge of metal detectors was thin, at best, but even with his limited frame of reference, he could tell the piece of equipment cuffed to Chapman's arm was no ordinary treasure hunter's toy.

"It's my own design," Ellie told him, noting the direction of his gaze. "Remember that little black box that contained the database I developed after those summers at Glorietta Pass?"

"Yes."

"It's a duplicate of the one that fits right here, on the neck of the metal dectector."

She signaled Chapman to raise the instrument for Jack's inspection. Grunting, the grad student lifted the heavy wand to waist level.

"I call this baby Discoverer Two," she said with a touch of proprietary pride. "Discoverer One was the prototype."

Like most metal sweepers, Discoverer came with a large, flat disk at the bottom end of its arm. At the top, where the wearer could comfortably read it, sat the computerized brain box Ellie referred to.

"One ping gives you a good idea of what you've found," Chapman added. "A low tone indicates iron, gold and nickel. A medium tone, lighter metals like aluminum pull tabs and zinc. Brass, copper and silver return a high pitch."

"In addition to the type of metal found," Ellie elaborated, "Discoverer will tell you how deep it's buried. The built-in computer also uses the signal return to paint a picture of the object here on this little screen. When we lock on something that looks, sounds and smells like a shell casing, the pre-programmed data from my prior research gives us a pretty good indication what type."

His arm sagging with the weight of the wand, Chapman waited patiently for her to finish describing some of the more technical aspects of the equipment. Once the grad student had trotted off to begin his sweeps, Ellie drew in a deep breath, braced herself and plunged into the shade of the cottonwoods.

The rest of her crew was there, doing their best to dodge the questions of a news reporter with a waist-length curtain of black hair and an air of dogged inquisitiveness. Sam Pierce stood solidly in front of the camera and greeted Ellie's arrival with barely disguised relief.

"Here's Dr. Alazar now. She can give you a better estimate of when we'll release our findings."

Jack stepped to the side and out of the picture as the camera locked onto Ellie.

"Dr. Alazar. Deborah Li, Channel Six news. We understand you've sent bit of bone from the remains you recovered to the police lab for DNA sampling."

"That's correct."

"When will you have the results?"

"Hopefully, by the end of the week."

"Then you're going to run a match against a sample from one of William Travis's descendents?"

"A great-great-grandniece has volunteered a sample," she confirmed. "So have descendents of several other Alamo defenders."

After all the bad press, Ellie only hoped the donors would still provide the samples as promised. Several had already voiced doubts. She didn't share that bit of information with the reporter, however.

"What if there's no match?" Li asked. "Pardon the pun, but won't that shoot your theory that the remains might belong to William Barrett Travis all to heck?"

"At this point, it's only a theory," she reminded the reporter with unruffled calm. "One of several we're working. If you like, I'll show you around the site. There's not much to see at this point, though," she warned. "We're almost finished here. By next

week, we hope to switch from field to full laboratory
mode.''

As curious as the reporter, Jack trailed along. It
was quite an operation, he discovered. Two vans held
racks for the team's equipment, which included an
impressive array of computers, field microscopes,
digital imaging cameras and chemicals for sampling
soil, wood and metal fragments. The excavation site
was cut into the bank of the creek. It formed a flat,
level bed where what looked like a hundred or so
cubic yards of mud and debris had been removed bit
by careful bit.

''As I said, there not much to see at this point.
The major artifacts we recovered have been photographed, catalogued and shipped to Baylor University, where Dr. Dawes-Hamilton and her assistants
will complete the authentication process. The skeletal
remains were transported to the San Antonio morgue
pending DNA identification and possible burial by
family. If we make no ID, the bishop of the diocese
has agreed they should be buried here, in San Jose's
old mission cemetery.''

At this point, Ellie explained, the team was working the final phase of on-site activity. Reconfirming
exact coordinates of the finds. Digging additional exploratory sites up and downstream to make sure they
hadn't missed any artifacts. Making last, expanded
sweeps with the metal detector.

Jack found the excavations fascinating, the decisive authority Ellie projected even more so. She was at once coolly professional and vibrantly passionate about her work. She never allowed the reporter to throw her off stride or pull information she preferred not to give.

When the news crew departed a half hour later, her skin wore a pearly sheen of perspiration and her boots were caked with mud, but no one viewing her on the news tonight could doubt her credentials or the intellectual honesty she brought to the project.

Not that either would protect her from a nut bent on safeguarding his preferred version of history. Or a professional hired for the same purpose.

His senses on full alert, Jack turned his attention to the group who remained after the TV crew departed. In addition to the professional members of the team, a number of amateur archeologists, high school students and interested volunteers had turned out to help.

"We don't have as many volunteers as we did at the start of the project," Ellie explained. "As a result of the adverse publicity, a number have defected."

Those who hadn't were already hard at work. As Jack soon discovered, even the last stages of fieldwork involved labor-intensive effort. He wasn't quite sure how Ellie roped him into it, but by mid-morning he was up to his knees in creek mud, digging an exploratory site alongside Sam Pierce and a fresh-faced sophomore.

Later that afternoon, he tried a turn with the metal detector. It took a few swipes to get into a smooth rhythm, keeping the bottom flat to the ground and the swing in a controlled arc. It also took muscle power. The contraption weighed only about eight or ten pounds, but felt more like twenty or thirty after Jack had covered the length of the compound's south wall a half dozen times.

True to Eric Chapman's predictions, the digital displays lit up like fireworks at any hint of metal. The number and variety óf objects buried beneath the earth astounded Jack. Discoverer Two hit on bridle bits, nails and barrel hoops from the nineteenth century, beer cans, bobby pins and dimes from the twentieth, and just about everything in between. His prize find was a blackened, dented silver disk.

"It's a concho," Ellie informed him after scrutinizing the object. "From the size of it, I'd say it's most likely off a bridle or sombrero. The concho was the decoration of choice on hats favored by both Mexicans and Tejanos. At least until a New Jersey hatter by the name of Stetson traveled west for his health and produced his version of the ten-gallon hat."

"I always wondered if those things really held ten gallons," Jack mused, recalling once again the Westerns he'd seen, where scouts and cowboys poured precious canteen water into their hats for their panting ponies.

Smiling, Ellie shook her head. "Only about three, actually, although that had nothing to do with the name. Gallon is a derivation of the Spanish word *galon,* which means braid. A ten-gallon hat simply refers to the amount of braiding around the brim."

"Another Hollywood myth shot down in flames," Jack muttered, shaking his head as she added the metal disk to the inventory of historical artifacts to be turned over to the National Park Service.

All too aware that they were working on borrowed time, the team remained at the dig until seven that evening. Once back at the hotel, Ellie conducted a quick wrap-up before sending her crew off to hit the showers and find dinner.

Jack was ready for both. When he knocked on the connecting door a half hour later, his stomach rumbled like a '56 Chevy with bad pipes. His hunger took on a whole different edge, however, when Ellie answered his knock. She'd changed into a long, gauzy flowered skirt in shades of green and lavender, topped by a lilac scoop-necked top. A silver crucifix on a thin chain circled her neck. Silver hoops dangled from her ears. As always, Jack noted with a kick to his gut, the bracelet he'd given her so many years ago banded her wrist.

But it was her hair that drew his gaze. She'd caught it back with combs at either temple and left the still damp, shining mass to tumble down her back, the way she used to when they'd first met.

Like hard right jabs, the memories hit him. Of tugging those combs free. Burying his face in that fragrant mass. Tunneling his fingers through the silky curtain to bring her mouth down to his.

Christ!

Clenching his fists, Jack managed to ask in a relatively normal voice where she wanted to have dinner.

"After last night's fiasco with room service, I suggest we go downstairs. Or better yet, out on the Riverwalk. I'll take you to my favorite Mexican restaurant. It's only a block away."

"Lead the way."

As Ellie had indicated, Casa del Rio was only a short walk from the hotel. They could have covered the distance in five minutes if not for the crowds jamming the popular Riverwalk.

"I've never seen it this packed," she told Jack as they took the stairs down to the river and plunged into the ebb and flow.

Crowded was an understatement. Tourists strolled shoulder-to-shoulder along the stone walks lining both sides of the placid green waterway. Many toted plastic drink cups and called to friends on the opposite side of river, pitching their voices to be heard over the music that spilled from the hotels and outdoor restaurants crowding the flagstone walk. A good number of the revelers wore wide-brimmed sombreros. Unlike the hats Jack and Ellie had discussed only this afternoon, these were cheap straw imitations decorated with red and green pom-poms instead of leather braid or silver conchos.

"There must be a convention in town," Ellie murmured, surveying the sea of straw.

"There is."

The comment came from a tourist decked out in an ankle-length red sundress and one of the distinctive sombreros. Dipping her head, she pointed to the lettering on the high-peaked crown.

"The American Travel Agents Association annual convention. Tonight's our big opening gala. You'll see the fireworks shooting up from the convention center later on."

Smiling her thanks, Ellie wedged sideways to make way for the woman and her companions. The movement brought her close to the river. Too close. Her heel caught on the edge.

"Careful!"

Jack's hand whipped out and caught her arm. He spun her away from the murky water. She landed awkwardly against his chest. Fingers splayed against his shirtfront, she blinked at him.

Ellie had never believed the silly cliché about time standing still, but for some reason the moment seemed to stretch forever. She could feel Jack's heat and the strong, steady beat of his heart under her fingertips. Her pulse skipped a beat, two, then drummed like thunder in her ears.

She didn't expect the hunger that leaped up and grabbed her by the throat. Wasn't prepared for it. Yet everything in her burst into a fever of need.

"Jack…"

He must have felt it, too. His muscles tensed. The arm he'd slipped around her waist to steady her tightened to a steel band. Ellie strained against him, aching, wanting, only to crash back to reality at the sound of a chuckle.

"Excuse us, folks. Hate to intrude on your little tête-à-tête, but we need to get by. Don't want to be late for the opening gala."

A glance over her shoulder showed a circle of grinning travel agents. Her cheeks warming, Ellie pulled out of Jack's arms. "Sorry."

"No apologies necessary, sweetie!" The woman in the red knit sundress laughed and let her gaze drift over Jack with unabashed feminine appreciation. "If a world-class hottie looked as hungry for me as this one just did for you, I sure as heck wouldn't be sorry."

Her glance dropped to Ellie's left hand. Grinning, she dug into her straw tote.

"Here's my card. Give me a call when you two are ready to make it legal, and I'll get you a heck of a deal on a honeymoon package."

Ellie's cheeks went from warm to downright hot

as she accepted the card the woman pressed on her and slipped it into her skirt pocket. Mute, she steered through the crowds toward the restaurant.

Jack kept his jaw clamped shut and his hand on Ellie's arm. *Not* because he couldn't bring himself to let her go. And certainly not because the press of her body against his for those brief moments had set spark to a fire in his belly he was doing his damnedest to douse.

The fact was he didn't like these crowds. Liked even less the advantage the restaurants and hotels on either side of the walkway gave a shooter. Anyone could check into the Hyatt or Hilton. Take a room on one of the upper floors. Line up a clear shot at the merrymakers flowing by below. His nerves crawling, Jack tucked Ellie closer to his side. She frowned when their hips bumped a time or two, but said nothing.

The restaurant she'd selected didn't provide any better cover. Case del Rio sat right on a bend of the river, its open-air patio a kaleidoscope of umbrellas and colored lights strung from tree to tree.

"Let's eat inside," Jack muttered, guiding Ellie away from the exposed patio and into the air-conditioned interior. Only after the waiter had showed them to a booth set well away from the windows and he'd scoped out the clientele did he allow his shoulders to slump against the back of the booth.

Ellie's brown eyes met his. He knew she'd felt it,

too. The way his muscles leaped under her touch. The instant heat every time they came in contact. He read the question in her eyes but didn't have an answer that would satisfy either one of them. He thought he caught a flash of disappointment, maybe even regret, before she picked up the menu and used it as a shield between them.

"I'll have combination number three," she told the waiter who plopped down a basket of chips and cups of salsa. "And a margarita."

"Same here," Jack said, tossing aside his menu. "No margarita, though. Just water."

"Just water?" Ellie echoed when the waiter departed. "As I recall, your drink of choice used to be an icy cold Corona."

"It still is, but not while I'm on duty."

"That's right." Frowning, she stabbed a chip into the salsa. "How could I forget? You're on duty."

The word hung between them, as solid as a brick wall and twice as impenetrable. In her last, furious tirade all those years ago, Ellie had accused him of caring more about the Corps than he did about her. Of letting his sense of duty take precedence over what they had together. What they could have together.

Like an uninvited guest who wouldn't take the hint and leave, the echoes of that ugly argument stayed at the table all through the meal. As a result, conversation was stilted, at best. Ellie shook her head when the waiter asked if she wanted another margarita, then abruptly changed her mind.

By the time she slurped up the last of her drink and they left the restaurant, dusk had softened to night, and colored lights twinkled all along the river. The late hour hadn't diminished the foot traffic. If anything, the crowds had increased. Barges filled with sightseers jammed hip-to-hip floated over the dark water. From another barge, a mariachi band poured a soaring rendition of ''Una Paloma Blanca'' into the night. The music drew cheers and applause from the appreciative crowd, most of whom, Jack noted, sported straw sombreros. The travel agents had descended on the Riverwalk en masse.

His muscles tensed in instinctive response to the crowd. Throngs like this could provide an excellent protective shield. Conversely, they could also mask the approach of unfriendlies.

Jack kept Ellie on the inside, away from the river, and forged a path toward the stairs leading up to street level. They were just a few feet from the steps when he heard a muted pop and the crack of rock splintering.

He took Ellie down in one swift lunge, covering her body with his on the way down. Before they hit the ground, the night exploded around them.

Chapter 7

Pinning Ellie to the stone, Jack yanked out his automatic and twisted around. In the heart-pounding seconds that followed, he registered the startled faces of tourists. The lights strung through the trees. The deafening booms that exploded into starbursts of glittering red and green.

"Hey!" one of the bystanders exclaimed over the flashes of color. "What the heck do you think you're doing?"

With a snarl, Jack whipped his weapon toward the source of the shout. The man's face went chalk white beneath his sombrero. Stumbling against his companions, he jerked up both palms.

"Take it easy, pal! Take it easy!"

There was another earsplitting series of pops. Red and green balloons pinwheeled through the sky. As the sound faded, Ellie gasped and wiggled under the dead weight pinning her to the flagstones.

"What's going on?"

Jack didn't take his eyes from the crowd. "I heard a gunshot."

"That—that was the fireworks," the white-faced travel agent stuttered, his hands still high. "Really, pal, all you heard was the fireworks."

As if to add emphasis to his nervous explanation, another series of booms exploded right overhead. Rockets of brilliant red and green shot into the night sky, trailing long, sparkling tails. A chorus of oohs and ahs rose from the spectators not engaged in the small drama occurring at the foot of the stairs.

"Jack." Ellie panted, wiggling frantically. "Please! I can't breathe."

He had to get her out of here. The single thought hammered in Jack's head. He rolled to his feet, the automatic tight against his thigh. Wrapping his free hand around Ellie's arm, he hauled her up.

The travel agent and his friends gaped as Jack hustled Ellie up the stone stairs. She was panting when they gained street level and decidedly unhappy when they arrived at the Menger. While the elevator whizzed them upward, she collapsed against the brass cage.

"That's twice now you've pulled that gun and

scared the dickens out of me. Tell me you haven't gone all Rambo since leaving the Marines.''

"I haven't gone all Rambo.''

"Then what's with the rather dramatic reaction to a few fireworks?''

"I recognize the sound of a gunshot fired from a silenced weapon when I hear it.''

Ellie opened her mouth, snapped it shut again. She didn't say a word during the walk down the hall to her room or while Jack checked the intrusion detection devices he'd set when they left the hotel. Satisfied no one had been in the rooms, he turned to face her.

She stood in the middle of the room, hugging her crossed arms. Her face and throat showed a decided pallor against the soft lilac of her top.

"If you did hear a gunshot,'' she said slowly, "it was timed perfectly to go off with the fireworks.''

"That's what I'm thinking.''

"So if there *was* a shooter, he's not some nutcase trying to scare me away.'' A shudder rippled down her body. Her fingers dug into her arms, making white marks in the tanned skin. "He's planning each move.''

As much as Jack wanted to shield her from the ugly suspicions he'd been harboring for the past twenty-four hours, he knew he had to level with her. She wasn't the young girl he'd once dreamed of keeping safe and warm in his arms. She was Dr.

Elena Maria Alazar, the woman he'd been sent to protect. As such, she had to understand the nature of the threat as he perceived it.

"I think we're dealing with a pro, Ellie. Someone who knows exactly what he's doing."

Briefly, he related the information he'd received from Mackenzie yesterday. Ellie's eyes narrowed as he detailed the assumed identity, the gunpowder residue, the Expedition carefully wiped clean of all prints.

"Why didn't you tell me all this before now?"

"I should have," he admitted.

She was furious, as she had every right to be. Eyes spitting fire, she marched up to him and jabbed a blunt-tipped finger into his chest.

"I'd suggest you remember who hired you, Carstairs."

"Your uncle, I was told."

"Wrong!" Her finger struck again. "Uncle Eduardo insisted I have a bodyguard. I insisted it be you."

"You were behind this job?" His hand closed over hers, stilling it before she could take another jab. "Why?"

"I felt guilty."

"Guilty?" That threw him. "For what?"

"For causing you to be sent home in disgrace," she snapped. "For ruining your military career. For making you start over as a hired hand with some obscure company no one's ever heard of.''

Jack couldn't tell her OMEGA worked very hard at remaining obscure. He was still absorbing the fact that Ellie had carried around a load of guilt all these years almost equal to his own.

''None of what happened was your fault,'' he countered fiercely. ''I knew the risks when I took you to bed. Given the same circumstances, I'd do it again. In a heartbeat.''

Her breath caught. She stared at him, her anger suspended, her hand fisting into a tight ball under his.

''What about—?''

She stopped. Drew her tongue along her lower lip. Forced out a ragged question.

''What about *these* circumstances?''

Jack barely swallowed his groan. He wanted her. God, he wanted her! The hunger was like a wild beast, clawing at his insides to get out.

This time there was more at stake than his career and her reputation, though. This time, her life might well depend on his ability to remain detached and alert.

''As you said, I'd best remember I'm a hired hand. I was sent here to protect you, Ellie.''

Disgust flickered in her eyes. Or was it disappointment? Before Jack could decide, she yanked her hand free of his.

"We've already had this discussion."

"Yes, we have."

"Do you have anything else to tell me about this phantom who may or may not be stalking me?"

"I wish I did."

She nodded. One quick, regal dip of her chin. "Then if you'll excuse me, I have work to do."

Jack took the hint and beat an orderly retreat. Somehow, he'd come out on the losing end of this discussion.

Ellie paced the sitting room, glaring at the computer sitting on the table, at the stacks of field notes waiting for review, at the closed connecting doors. Despite her icy request that Jack make himself scarce, work was the farthest thing from her mind at the moment.

What was the matter with her! Hadn't she learned her lesson nine years ago? Why in the world was she twisting herself into knots like this?

Over Jack Carstairs, for pity's sake! The stubborn Marine who'd considered her too young, too starry-eyed, to know her own mind. The noble idiot who'd walked away from her. The man who'd already broken her heart once.

If she let him do it again, she'd be a fool! A total, one-hundred-percent, feather-headed fool!

No way was she giving in to the heat that had flamed under her skin at his touch. *Or* following up

on his startling admission that he'd take her to bed
again in a heartbeat, given the same circumstances.

She had herself convinced, completely convinced,
until she shoved her hands in the pockets of her skirt
and felt a slip of pasteboard. Her throat tightening,
she pulled out the business card the travel agent had
pressed on her earlier. She stared at the embossed
printing until it blurred. Crumpling the card in her
fist, she whirled, crossed the room and yanked open
the connecting doors.

Jack was standing at the window, hands shoved in
his back pockets, staring out at the darkness. Her
abrupt entrance spun him around.

"I have to know." She bit the words out. "Did
you ever love me?"

"What?"

"Tell me, dammit. Did you love me?"

So bad, he'd hurt with it. In every inch of his body.
Jack couldn't admit the truth then. And it was too
late now. Far too late.

"What difference does it make?" he said quietly.
"What's done is done."

"Bull!" She flared up, as fiery and passionate as
the girl he'd once known. "It makes all the difference in the world. I want to know. I need to know."

"What you need is to go back to your room before
one of us says something we might regret."

"Like what?" She advanced on him, her chin
tipped to an angle he recognized all too well. "That

we still want each other? That you get still hard and I still get hot every time we bump knees or hips or elbows?''

''Ellie, for Christ's sake!''

''What? Are you worried I'll bring up the fact that you wanted to kiss me down there on the river before dinner? Or admit that I *ached* for you to do it?''

She stopped in front of him. Her breasts rose and fell under the scoop-necked top. A pulse beat wildly in one side of her throat.

''I'm still aching, Jack.''

Her total honesty humbled him, just as it had nine years ago. She held nothing back. She never had. Desire jolted into him, as hot and fierce as any he'd ever felt for her. He went rigid, fighting the shock, fighting himself.

Ellie couldn't miss his reaction. Triumph leaped into her eyes. She moved closer, determined to get at the truth whether he wanted it out or not.

''I have to know.''

She raised her arms, slid them around his neck. Her breasts flattened against his chest. Her hips canted, pressing her belly into the bulge that pushed hard and hurting against his zipper.

''Did you love me?''

He couldn't lie to her. He'd never lied to her. But neither could he fully articulate the tangle of emotions she'd roused in him. He hesitated for long moments, then offered her the only answer he could.

"I would have laid down my life for you."

Her throat closed. He *had* laid down his life for her. The only real life he'd ever known. At the same time, he'd spurned her offer to do the same.

"But you wouldn't let me sacrifice my reputation or my career for you."

His jaw locked. "That was different."

She stared at him, torn between a sharp, sudden urge to whack him alongside the head and the over-whelming need to kiss the mule-headed stubbornness right off his face.

She waffled between the contradictory impulses for several moments before muttering a curse that would have shocked her students and her colleagues. Tightening her arms, she hauled herself up on her toes and fastened her mouth on his.

Jack stood stiff and unyielding under her assault, but he didn't break the contact. He didn't even *try* to break the contact. Her pulse leaping, Ellie angled her head to fit her mouth more fully against his.

Memories of other nights and other kisses exploded inside her head. Deliberately she blanked her mind and concentrated fiercely on this moment.

When she finally pulled away, Jack might have been carved from gray Texas granite. His jaw was set. The cords in his neck stood out in stark relief. His blue eyes were dark, shuttered, hiding his thoughts.

Ellie felt the first twinge of remorse, followed

swiftly by self-disgust. She'd done it again! Thrown herself at the man. Shame coursed through her, but pride kept her head high as she offered a stiff apology.

"I'm sorry, Jack. That was stupid of me. I had no business complicating an already awkward situation."

His stony silence signaled complete agreement.

Ellie forced a smile. "You'd think I'd have learned to exercise some restraint in nine years."

Actually, she had. She'd acquired a good deal of patience and restraint. She'd dated a fair number of men over the years. Had even thought she could fall in love with one or two. Yet she'd never *attacked* any of them.

Only Jack.

God, she was such a fool!

"I'm sorry," she whispered once again.

Writhing inside, she kept the smile plastered on her face and her chin high as she turned and headed for the connecting doors.

Let her walk.

The words thundered in Jack's head. He had to let her walk. If his years of experience as an undercover operative hadn't already underscored the need to maintain a clear head, Lightning had laid the issue square on the line. Jack was to keep his mind on the mission and his hands off Ellie. Period. End of discussion.

She got one step, maybe two, before he made a sound halfway between a snarl and a curse and went after her. Snagging her elbow, he yanked her around.

''We can both be sorry.''

The force of his kiss bent her backward. For a moment, Ellie thought her spine might crack. Recovering from her startled surprise, she threw her arms around his neck and fit her body to his.

Unleashed, his hunger was like a live, ravaging beast. It devoured Ellie. Consumed her. Thrilled her to her core.

This was a different Jack, she thought on a rush of wild excitement. Not the tender, passionate lover who'd teased and tormented her. Not the skilled tutor who'd schooled her in pleasures she'd never imagined. This Jack made no attempt to disguise what he wanted.

Ellie.

Naked.

Under him.

Afterward, she could never say who dragged whom down to the plush carpet. All she knew was that she was on fire by the time they hit. Every inch of her body flamed with heat. The areas Jack paid special, savage attention to blazed white-hot. Her lips. Her breasts. Her belly. The tight, aching nub between her thighs.

He stripped off her clothes first, then his own, all

the time doing things to her that had Ellie alternating between groans and breathless little pants.

She didn't lay passive. Submissiveness didn't form any part of her character. Her hands kept as busy as his. So did her mouth and tongue and teeth. Awash in a sea of sensations, she rediscovered the texture of his skin, the wiry tickle of his chest hair, the satin-smooth heat of his engorged shaft.

When he worked his hand between her thighs, she was wet and ready. So ready. Still, he primed her. The heel of his hand exerted exquisite, maddening pressure on her mound. His fingers worked a steady rhythm inside her. Ellie stood it as long as she could before lifting her body in a taut arc.

"Jack! Now!"

"No." Deliberately, he eased the tormenting pressure. "Not yet, Ellie. I've laid awake too many nights remembering how you—"

With a muttered curse, he bit off the rest of the sentence. A red flush mounted his cheeks.

Stunned, Ellie stared at the rugged planes of his face. He'd thought about her. Dreamed about her. Laid awake remembering her touch and her taste. The realization melted away the years. With them went much of the long-buried hurt and anger.

"I've laid awake, too," she whispered. "Too many nights to count."

His eyes searched hers. His jaw was clenched so tight Ellie thought it might crack. Just when she

thought she'd have to take the initiative again, he
groped for his jeans. For an awful moment, she
thought he'd changed his mind. Frustration and chagrin welled to fill her throat with a taste like chalk.

To her infinite relief, he'd only paused to dig a
condom out of his wallet. He'd protected her all
those years ago, she remembered on a warm rush of
emotion. He was still protecting her.

He sheathed himself with quick, jerky strokes,
then rolled back to her. One hand tangled in her hair,
bringing her head up for his crushing kiss. The other
parted her legs and positioned his rigid member. Ellie
opened for him joyously, eagerly, her heart singing
a welcome even as her hips lifted to meet his initial
thrust.

They made love with all the fury and twice the
skill of their youth.

The first time was fast and hard. Mouths greedy,
hands groping, hips grinding, they rolled over and
over on the plush carpet. Ellie climaxed twice, mind-
shattering orgasms that left her whimpering. Jack
held back as long as he could, determined to draw
out their pleasure, until Ellie took matters out of his
hands. Hooking a leg, she climbed astride him,
wrapped her fingers around his shaft and held him
steady as she sank down, inch by satiny inch.

The second time was slower, lazier and took place

in bed, thank goodness. Ellie knew she'd sport a nice complement of carpet burns in the morning.

The third time left her completely sated and limp with exhaustion. It was well past midnight when she fell asleep, her arm flung across Jack's chest and her nose buried in his neck.

She awoke the next morning to find him sitting in the chair across the room. He was dressed all in black, unshaven, and looked more dangerous than she'd ever imagined he could.

Chapter 8

One glance at Jack's tight jaw and grim expression sent a single thought ripping through Ellie's sleep-fuzzed mind.

He was going to leave. Again.

With a flash of pure pain, she sensed that he was already regretting last night. As he'd pointed out several times, he was there to protect her. Only to protect her. Getting involved with Elena Maria Alazar—again—compromised not only his ability to do his job, it could very well cost him the career he'd carved out since leaving the Marine Corps.

Her chest squeezed so hard and tight she could barely breathe. Yanking at the tangled sheet, she bunched it over her breasts and wiggled up to rest her bare shoulders against the wrought-iron headboard. With some effort, she managed to keep her crushing sense of loss out of her voice.

"You're already dressed, I see. Are you going out?"

"I've been out."

"Have you? Where?"

Her cool, almost disinterested query irritated the hell out of Jack. He'd spent three hellacious hours, first down at the river, searching for proof that someone had, in fact, fired at Ellie last night, then convincing the San Antonio PD detective honchoing her case to haul his butt out of bed. Jack wanted a cast of the fresh scar he'd found in the stone steps. Maybe ballistics could turn up information as to the type of bullet that had gouged it.

Finding evidence that a killer had taken aim at Ellie was bad enough. Seeing her naked and sleepy-eyed, sporting what looked suspiciously like a whisker burn on the curve of her left shoulder, magnified Jack's self-disgust and guilt a hundred times over.

He'd been sent to San Antonio to keep her safe, for God's sake! And what the hell did he do? Spent half the night rolling around in the sack with the woman whose life might well depend on his focus and ability to concentrate.

If the killer had tried again...

If he'd hit when Jack was otherwise occupied...

If Ellie had been hurt...

His gut twisting, he practically snarled at her. "I told you I recognized the sound of a round fired from a silenced gun when I heard one."

She looked confused for a moment, either at his savage tone or the information he'd imparted.

"Last night," he growled, "on the Riverwalk, right when the fireworks went off. That was a shot."

The fingers gripping the bunched sheet went white at the knuckles. "Are you sure?"

"I'm sure. I found the gouge in the stone where the bullet hit."

The last of the sleepy flush left her cheeks. She stared at Jack, her eyes wide with dismay. Speculating that they might or might not have heard a gunshot was one thing, he knew. Having the brutal fact confirmed was another.

He hated the fleeting look of fear and helplessness that chased across her face. Hated even more driving home the fact that she was a target.

"From the angle of the mark," he continued tersely, "it looks like the shell ricocheted off the stone into the river. Detective Harris and an SAPD crime scene crew are down there now, trying to locate the shell and run it through ballistics."

Some of the helpless vulnerability left her face. "I can help with that! I'll lay odds my team's equipment is considerably more sophisticated than the police department's."

Dragging the sheet with her, she swung her legs over the edge of the mattress and groped for her clothes. Jack's harsh voice stopped her cold.

"Someone wants you dead, Ellie. Very dead. You're not leaving this room until I find out who."

"But..."

"The matter's not open for discussion or debate. Just so you know, I've requested backup to augment your security detail. I've also called in an expert from the company I work for to provide additional electronic surveillance and defensive countermeasures. Both team members are en route as we speak."

"Jack, be reasonable. I can't just cower here in my hotel room. Ballistics is my area of expertise. I can help. I want to help."

"I told you, the issue's not up for negotiation."

Her chin went up. "I'm not negotiating. Give me ten minutes to shower and dress."

Scooping up her clothes, she yanked the tail ends of the sheet free of the mattress and headed for the bathroom. Jack spit out a curse and followed. The shower jets were already turned to full blast when he pushed inside.

Her clothes lay in a scattered heap on the tile, along with the discarded sheet. Whirling, she snatched a towel from the nearest rack. Jack had a feeling he'd carry the image of her copper-tipped breasts, flat belly and the dark, seductive triangle between her legs around in his head for a long, long time.

"I said ten minutes!"

"And I said you're not going anywhere."

Steam curled through the open stall door. The jets drummed against the glass. Ellie made a heroic attempt at calm and reasonable. And failed.

"I'm not one of your troops. You don't bark orders at me and expect unquestioned obedience. I'm an expert in my field, just as you are in yours. I'm going to—"

"You're going to stay where I put you."

"*Put* me?"

"Don't force me take extreme measures."

Scorn flashed in her eyes. "What are you going to do? Lock me in the bathroom?"

"I was thinking more along the lines of handcuffing you to the bed."

"Oh, give me a break! I know you too well, Carstairs. You wouldn't resort to such Neanderthal tactics."

His gaze raked her near-naked form. A grim smile settled in his eyes.

"Oh, yeah, babe. I would."

Without warning, the tension in the steam-filled bathroom took on a whole different edge. Ellie felt it right down to her bones. A sudden wariness that had nothing to do with bullets or ballistics sent her back a step. A feminine instinct older than time screamed at her to cover herself, placate the angry male before her, defuse the situation.

Being Ellie, she did just the opposite. Another instinct, sharp and urgent, demanded she stand her ground. This was Jack, she reminded herself furiously. She'd let his hardheadedness defeat her once. She couldn't let him ride roughshod over her again. Not if she wanted him to consider her his equal. In *and* out of bed.

Spray from the open shower enveloped her in a fine mist. Steam invaded her lungs. Blinking away the drops that had collected on her lashes, Ellie looked him square in the eye.

"I wouldn't mind doing the bed-and-handcuff bit, as long as we take turns as the cuffee. But not right now, Jack. Right now I'm going to take a shower, get dressed and haul myself and my equipment down to the river. You can accept my decision and come with me, or..."

She let the sentence trail off, stalling for time while she tried to decide just what the heck *or* she could throw at him.

Jack obviously had a few ideas of his own. His eyes narrowed. The hot mist had soaked his hair and raised a sheen on the stubble darkening his cheeks. He looked wet and angry and menacing as he took a step forward.

"Or what, Ellie? You'll fire me?"

''Oh, no! I'm not letting you walk away from me again.''

The retort spilled out before she could stop it. Recklessly, Ellie laid the rest of her tumultuous emotions on the line.

''We started something last night, Carstairs. Correction, we *restarted* something. I for one think we should see it thought to the finish this time.''

Her heart slamming against her ribs, she waited to hear Jack's take on the matter. He declined to give one. Instead, he spun on one heel and made for the bathroom door.

Ellie's toes curled into the tiles. Fury and pain lanced into her in equal measures. ''Jack! Dammit, you can't just—''

''Someone's at the door.'' He threw the words over his shoulder. ''I'll see who it is, then we'll finish this discussion.''

She hadn't heard a thing over the pelting water and the heat of her emotions. Muttering under her breath, she kicked the bathroom door shut, then stepped into the shower stall. When they finished this discussion, she wouldn't be bare-assed and still sticky with the residue of their lovemaking.

When he peered through the peephole and identified the individual on the other side of the door, Jack didn't know whether to curse or give a heartfelt grunt of relief. He settled for twisting the dead bolt and greeting OMEGA's chief of communications with a curt acknowledgment.

"You got here fast."

"Lightning put his personal jet at our disposal."

Mackenzie Blair breezed in, toting her heavy field case. She wore the uniform she favored for traveling, Jack noted: a dark blue T-shirt emblazoned with U.S. Navy in four-inch gold letters, snug jeans and serious running shoes. Few of OMEGA's special agents could keep up with the woman when she hit her stride.

She'd have a full assortment of other garments in her case, Jack knew. He and the other males at OMEGA all harbored a particular partiality for the jumpsuit she slipped into for night operations. The black nylon zipped up to her chin and covered her slender curves like a thin coat of paint.

Taking a quick glance around the suite, she cocked her head at the sound of running water in the other room. "Did I get you out of the shower?"

"No."

One brow lifted. "There must be some other reason your clothes are soaked, then."

There was, but Jack didn't offer it. His black shirt sticking to him like wet saran, he closed the door to the suite. Mackenzie dumped her case on a handy chair and turned to face him.

"Cyrene is checking in downstairs. I came right up. I've got something for you, Renegade."

Jack's pulse jumped at the intense satisfaction glimmering in her eyes.

"We IDed some interesting characters in our screen of Dr. Alazar's digital images. One in particular will catch your attention."

Punching in a code on the digital lock, she opened her field case and produced a flat silver CD. Her gaze cut to the computer sitting on the desk.

"Will Dr. Alazar mind if I use her laptop?"

Jack shook his head, although at this point he couldn't predict Ellie's reactions to anything. She'd put his back up with her stubborn resistance to his orders and thrown him for a complete loop with that business about not letting him walk away from her again.

Elena Maria obviously hadn't figured it out yet, but he had no intention of leaving her. Or letting her leave him. Not after last night. And sure as hell not with a killer stalking her.

His mouth set, he crossed the room to peer over Mackenzie's shoulder. She drummed her fingers impatiently while the laptop booted up, then sent them flying over the keys. A moment later, a scene was painted across the screen.

It was the courtyard of the Alamo. Jack recognized the low, flat building Ellie had identified as the Long Barracks in the foreground. In the background was the massive oak that gave welcome shade to the throngs of tourists wandering from exhibit to exhibit.

"There he is."

With a click of the mouse, Mackenzie placed an arrow on one particular tourist. He wore a straw Stetson and dark glasses. A camera was slung over one shoulder. He stood in the shade at the rear of the courtyard next to another man.

"It took me a while to ID him. The glasses obscure his eyes, and the hat conceals his hair color, although I doubt it's still the same color listed on the FBI most-wanted bulletin."

Well, hell! The FBI's most-wanted bulletin. That's all Jack needed to hear. The tension coiling his muscles took another tight twist.

"I finally got a hit on the scar." Clicking away, Mackenzie zoomed in on the man's profile. "See it? Just below his left ear?"

He saw it. "Unless I miss my guess, someone once took a knife to this particular tourist's throat."

"You pegged it. According to FBI reports, he got that little souvenir from a street pimp who strenuously objected to being taken out. He's a hit man, Renegade. A real professional. Suspected of killing at least ten people, both in the States and abroad."

Jack had suspected he was dealing with a pro. Knowing he was right didn't give him so much as a hint of satisfaction.

"The man's assumed dozens of different identities over the years," Mackenzie reported. "Including, we can lay odds, Mr. Harold Berger of 2224 Riverside

Drive, Austin. The FBI was *very* interested to hear he'd popped up in San Antonio. Particularly when we IDed the man standing next to him.''

She zinged the pointer to a beefy, wide-shouldered man with sandy hair and a bulldog jaw.

''Meet Mr. Dan Foster. He's local, a very successful building contractor.''

''What his connection to our hit man?''

''Three months ago, Foster's wife was kidnapped from their country club estate. Although there were some indications that both Fosters played around, Danny Boy appeared devastated by the kidnapping and insisted on paying the million-dollar ransom.''

Eyes narrowed, Jack studied the image on the screen. Despite his size, Foster gave off a definite country club air. A designer logo decorated the pocket of his knit shirt. His khaki Dockers showed a knife crease. Gold flashed at one wrist.

''Before Foster could get the funds together,'' Mackenzie continued, ''his wife's body turned up in a Dumpster. From the rope burns on her wrists and ankles, shredded nylons and gravel embedded in her knees, the FBI thinks she tried to escape and was shot in the process. Now, you'd expect the supposed kidnapper to bury the body or otherwise keep it hidden until after he'd collected the ransom.''

''Unless he *wanted* it found,'' Jack said slowly.

''Right. Again, our friend Foster appeared devastated. But the Feds took note of the fact that he was sole beneficiary on his wife's two-million-dollar life insurance policy. And that he was falling behind on repayment of several major business loans he'd floated.''

The pieces fell together with startling clarity. The trashing of Ellie's hotel room, her stolen computer, the attempts on her life. None of those had anything to do with the controversy she's stirred up in town, but with the fact she caught a killer and the man who could well have hired him on camera.

''Foster must have sweated blood when he read the stories about Ellie in the papers,'' Jack guessed. ''Particularly those that went into detail about her digital scans of the Alamo and its weaponry. It wouldn't have taken more than a few calls for Foster to find out if Dr. Alazar was at the Alamo the same day he arranged to meet Scarface there.''

''What I don't understand,'' Mackenzie said, tapping a finger on the keyboard, ''is why the heck they'd risk meeting in such a public place.''

''Maybe he didn't feel safe meeting with a killer anywhere else. Maybe Scarface insisted on it, intending to blackmail Foster later by threatening to reveal his shady connections.''

''Then why would he care if Dr. Alazar caught the meeting on camera?''

''Scarface might not care, but Foster sure as hell would. My guess is he hired the guy to trash Ellie's hotel room and destroy her digital images. When word got out she'd backed them up, Foster would have no choice but to take out a contract on Ellie, too, hoping her death would scuttle her project—and the pictures she'd taken—before they ever saw light of day.''

It was all speculation. Mere guesswork. But Jack knew in his gut they'd stumbled onto something.

"Did the Feds run a ballistics analysis of the bullet that killed Foster's wife?"

"I'm sure they did. I can e-mail my contact at the Bureau and find out. Why?"

"Because I'll bet you another dozen pizzas that the rifling marks on the bullet retrieved from her body will match those on the one fired at Ellie last night."

"Which makes it even more imperative we retrieve it from the river," a cool voice said behind them.

Jack grunted in disgust. Hell of a field agent he made! He hadn't heard the shower cut off. His only excuse was that Mackenzie's startling information had riveted his attention.

The new arrival seemed to rivet Mackenzie's. Her fascinated glance took in every detail of Ellie's fresh scrubbed face and damp hair before shifting to Jack's still wet shirt. OMEGA's chief of communications didn't say a word. She didn't have to. The deliberately bland expression she assumed said it all.

Unfortunately Lightning hadn't exercised the same

restraint. When Jack reported that matters between him and Ellie had taken an unexpected and very personal turn, Nick had ripped a foot-wide strip off his agent's hide.

Jack had expected nothing less. He'd also expected Lightning to yank him off the mission and was fully prepared to tell OMEGA's director to go to hell. No way Jack was leaving Ellie. He intended to stick so close to her she couldn't tell her shadow from his until he brought her stalker down.

After that...

His stomach clenched. He couldn't allow himself to think past right here, right now. Ellie's safety demanded his total focus. After would have to take care of itself. Silently, he watched her cross the room and hold out a hand to Mackenzie.

"I'm Elena Alazar. I assume you're one of Jack's colleagues."

"That's right."

Effortlessly, Mac slipped into the cover identity designed to shield her OMEGA connection. Since her extensive network of friends and acquaintances from her Navy days all knew about her background in and fascination with electronic gadgetry, she'd set up a fictitious company. Blair Consulting was listed in the Yellow Pages. It maintained a fancy home Page on the Web. Only a handful of Washington insiders knew the company's proprietor and sole employee worked exclusively for OMEGA.

"I'm Mackenzie Blair, Dr. Alazar. I own Blair Consulting. We specialize in electronic surveillance and computerized data searches. It's a pleasure to meet the woman who designed and developed the prototype for Discoverer Two."

"You know about metal detectors?"

"I'm former Navy," she answered with a grin. "We squids all harbor a secret fascination with sunken treasure. I've done my share of beachcombing."

"Then you might be interested in watching the Discoverer Two in action," Ellie said with a smile that did *not* include Jack. "I'm going to take it down to the river to help locate the shell casing you're both so interested in."

"Great!" Mackenzie enthused before Jack could counter Ellie's flat statement. "I'd love to see that sucker in operation. I understand you've loaded twenty gigabytes of metallurgical and ballistics data into its core operating system."

"Twenty-four, actually."

"Good Lord! How did you cram all that data in a portable device?"

"By compressing the reference files and—"

"Ladies," Jack interrupted. "Do you mind if we get back to the small matter of a stalker?"

Both women turned at his heavy-handed attempt to head off what had all the earmarks of an animated and lengthy discussion of bits and bytes.

''How much did you hear of what Mac had to say about the men in this image?'' he asked Ellie.

Her glance flicked to the screen. It lingered on Scarface for long moments before shifting to Foster.

''Enough to make me want to hurt those bastards,'' she said fiercely. ''Really bad. Let's get to work, shall we?''

Chapter 9

While Ellie and the young grad student on her team assembled the equipment she wanted to divert from the archeological site to the river, Jack met with the back-up agent OMEGA had sent in. Normally, Jack worked alone. The fact that he'd requested backup hadn't surprised Lightning, coming as it did on the heels of Renegade's admission that he'd crossed the line with Ellie.

After he'd finished tearing into Jack, Nick had sent one of the best. Claire Cantwell, code name Cyrene, had lost her husband to a bungled attempt to free a group of oil executives being held in Malaysia by radical separatists. Burying her grief behind a serene façade, she'd schooled herself to become one of the world's foremost experts on hostage negotiation. A noted psychologist, she was also OMEGA's most skilled agent when it came to screening crowds and identifying potential troublemakers.

Mackenzie respected and admired Renegade and Cyrene and looked forward to providing their on-scene electronics support. She'd just checked out a super-cool lie-detecting camera being developed by the Homeland Defense folks for airport use. The handy-dandy little device spotted deceivers by recording mild facial warming when under stress. She couldn't wait to have Cyrene test it out in her crowd surveillance. But when she checked into her room and made her initial on-site report, Lightning laid another task on her.

Nick Jensen's face was displayed with crystal clarity on the small screen of her communications unit. Thoughtful. A bit grim. And so damned handsome Mackenzie was tempted to drag her thumb over the trackball to blur the image a bit. She couldn't quite handle the combined impact of his navy blazer, Windsor-knotted red silk tie and deep tan this early in the morning!

"I want Foster on an electronic leash," Nick said. "He'd going to contact his hired gun sooner or later. He'll demand a progress report, or at least an explanation of why the hit's taking so long. Renegade will want to hear it when he does."

"No problem." Her mind was already sorting

through various technical options. "I'll look through my bag of tricks and see what we've got to play with."

"Good."

"Is that it?"

"For now."

"Roger."

Signing off, Mackenzie considered the best approach to Foster. Normally, field agents tagged targets. In fact, the unwritten rule of thumb was that *only* field agents made direct contact with targets. But Renegade needed Cyrene for backup on the river. There was no reason Mackenzie couldn't accomplish this little task herself.

The background dossier she'd compiled on Daniel Foster indicated he was something of a playboy who went in for the coy, kittenish type. She didn't have a kittenish bone in her body, and she wasn't sure how well she could do coy, but she'd give both her best shot.

Her first step was to trade her jeans and Nikes for strappy sandals and a sleeveless, V-neck dress with a matching short-sleeved jacket. The slinky black matte jersey defied wrinkles. It also clung to her slender curves.

After unclipping her hair, Mac dragged a brush through the shoulder-length dark mass and applied more makeup than she usually wore. A quick survey in the bathroom mirror convinced her to take a page from her mentor's book.

Maggie Sinclair, code name Chamelon, could assume a completely different personality with a few strategic accessories. At various times, Maggie had gone into the field disguised as a nun, a nuclear scientist and a high-priced call girl. On one memorable mission, she'd lifted a black lace garter belt and fishnet stockings from a shop, left a note for the owner to send the bill to the American consulate and waltzed into a smoke-filled waterfront dive that catered to gunrunners and drug lords.

What she needed, Mackenzie decided, was the equivalent of a black lace garter.

She found just what she was looking for at the department store located in the massive River Center complex adjacent to the Menger. The underwire demi-bra transformed even her modest curves into plump, seductive mounds. Additional pads pushed her breasts up so high they almost spilled out of the V-neck. More than satisfied with the result, Mackenzie charged the miracle bra to her OMEGA expense account.

She returned to the Menger and waited for the sporty little Mustang she'd arranged to have waiting at the south-side airport where Nick's private plane had landed this morning. The same valet who'd parked it in the Menger's garage less than an hour ago gawked at her dramatic cleavage when he delivered the vehicle curbside.

After she slid behind the wheel, Mackenzie placed her field case on the passenger seat and flipped down its side to access the keyboard. Dan Foster would be at work by now. According to the information she'd gleaned from her FBI contact, the two million Foster had collected from the insurance company after his wife's murder got him current on his construction company's outstanding loans but hadn't paid them off by any means. The man still had to work for a living.

She accessed the address and phone number of his office, then put in a quick call. The helpful receptionist informed her Mr. Foster was on-site at a job on San Antonio's north side. Twenty minutes later, Mackenzie pulled up at the fenced construction site.

Massive steel girders shot twenty-four stories into the cloudless blue sky. Super cranes hoisted beams to workers who appeared ant-like from the ground. Trucks raised clouds of dust as they rumbled in and out of the gate in the chain-link security fence.

Once again Mackenzie reached into her case. She peeled off the adhesive backing on a tiny, transparent disc, then stuck the disk to the back of her business card. Once attached, it became invisible. No one could tell it was there without a microscope.

She had just climbed out of the Mustang when two men exited the trailer parked beside the gate. One carried a clipboard and wore a badge identifying him as some kind of inspector.

The other was her quarry.

Her stomach did a little flip. Foster's size didn't intimidate her. Nor did his rugged good looks impress her. At all. It was just that the newspaper clippings and shots of Dan Foster the FBI had compiled did *not* do him justice.

Those grainy black-and-whites had depicted the man in a tux, his wife at his side, attending some fancy do at the country club. Or in a dark suit, his face contorted in grief as he exited a limo after her funeral.

This morning he was in boots, jeans and a hard hat. His rolled-up sleeves displayed trunklike arms that could only have been acquired by manhandling the dozers and cranes he now hired others to operate. Muscle had never particularly turned Mackenzie on, but she had to admit this guy's were impressive.

"Mr. Foster?"

He squinted through the dust. She started toward him, remembered her role and altered her stride to a hip-swinging glide.

"I'm Mackenzie Blair, president of Blair Consulting."

Foster accepted the business card she held out, but his glance made a detour to her chest and lingered for several seconds before dropping to examine the engraved lettering.

"I called your office for an appointment, but your secretary said you'd be on-site all day and suggested I catch you here."

"What can I do for you, Ms. Blair?"

"My consulting firm that specializes in electronic communications. I'm looking to expand my operations in this part of the country and would like to talk to you about the communications support you plan to put in this building."

"I've already accepted a bid from a subcontractor to wire it."

He was going with hard wire. Good. That gave her just opening she needed.

"I think you should consider fiber optics instead of wire."

"Well, I..."

"You'd be offering state-of-the-art networking capability to whoever occupies the building. And..." Her voice dropped to a throaty purr. "I guarantee I could save you a minimum of a hundred thousand dollars."

She'd pulled the figure out of a hat, a sheer guess based on the size of the project. As she'd anticipated, though, the combination of succulent Wonder curves and a possible hundred grand in savings proved irresistible.

The contractor's eyes gleamed under the rim of his hard hat. "A hundred thousand, huh?"

A teasing smile played at her lips. "I'm good at what I do, Mr. Foster."

"I'll just bet you are."

His glance dropped to her chest again before shifting to the inspector waiting patiently a few feet away.

"Look, I'm going to be tied up here for most of the day. Why don't we get together for a drink this evening and discuss all this money you're going to save me?"

Mackenzie let her smile curve into a seductive promise. "My cell phone number's on that business card. Call me."

"I will." Grinning, he tucked the card into his pocket and gave it a pat. "Talk to you tonight, Ms. Blair."

Oh, you'll be talking to me before then.

On that smug thought, she strolled to the Mustang.

A quarter mile from the site, she pulled to the side of the road and extracted a wireless earpiece. With the plastic piece tucked comfortably in her right ear, she keyed a special code into the receiver. Foster's angry voice stabbed into her head.

"…filed for those permits two months ago. I wish to hell you folks would get your act together."

Wincing, Mackenzie adjusted the volume. She'd tagged her target, temporarily at least. She'd replace the tag with a more permanent one tonight. Humming with satisfaction, she called in a quick order to

OMEGA's communications center to monitor the transmissions and drove off.

She connected with Renegade at the stairs leading to the Riverwalk. He'd planted both fists on the stone balustrade. His gaze was locked on the scene below.

The San Antonio PD had cordoned off a section of the river and commandeered one of the colorful river barges. Several uniformed and plainclothes police officers occupied the boat, which floated at the end of a long tether.

Dr. Alazar was in the barge, as well, along with her flame-haired assistant. As Mackenzie watched, Ellie slipped the heavy instrument that could only be Discoverer Two off her arm and passed it to the grad student.

"How's it going?" she asked the man beside her.

"It's not."

His face grim, Jack turned to give her a quick rundown. His startled glance zeroed in on her cleavage.

"Good Lord!"

"Hey, thanks a lot! At least Foster liked the new me."

Renegade's gaze whipped up to lock with hers. "You made contact?"

"And then some." Grinning, she tapped her ear. "He's right here, inside my head."

"Dammit, Mac, you shouldn't have tackled the

guy alone. You shouldn't have tackled him at all, for that matter. That's my job, or Cyrene's.''

"You were busy. And he was an easy mark. I'm a walking window into everything the man says or does. At the moment Danny Boy is... Hmm. It sounds like he's taking what we used to refer to in the Navy as a leak.''

"Has he talked to Scarface?"

"No. But he wants to continue *our* conversation. We're having drinks later tonight.''

"Does Lightning know about this?"

"Lightning's the one who said to tag the creep.''

She was stretching things a bit there. She knew it. Jack knew it.

"Last time I checked the field manual,'' he drawled, "tagging didn't include dinner or drinks.''

Since there was no such thing as a field manual for his line of work, Mackenzie decided to ignore the comment.

"Bring me up to speed on the salvage operation,'' she said instead, turning her attention to the barge. "What's happening?"

"Ellie laid out a search grid based on the angle of the gouge mark in the stone. They've been sweeping from left to right.'' Frustration edged his voice. "They're almost at the end of the grid.''

"They haven't found anything?"

"Are you kidding? They've found everything but the kitchen sink. That'll probably turn up, too. In the meantime, they've racked up an impressive collection of tire jacks, switchblades, car keys and coins in a dozen different currencies and denominations. But no bullets.''

"Hmm. Where's Cyrene?"

"Over there, at that restaurant. Second table to the left, by the rail."

Mackenzie spotted the pale-haired agent at the open-air restaurant on the opposite side of the river. The elevated deck gave the agent a bird's-eye view of the barge as well as the curious crowd that had gathered to watch. With Renegade and Cyrene flying cover, Mackenzie opted for a closer view of the action.

"I'm going down to watch. I want to see Discoverer Two up close and personal."

She had taken only a few steps before she heard a high-pitched pinging. Dr. Alazar's assistant gave an excited exclamation.

"I've got something on the screen! The digital displays indicate it's a spent forty-one caliber hollow-point casing, two hundred grain, number one hundred. Probably a Speer, although it could be a Remington.''

Brushing past Mackenzie, Jack went down the stone stairs two at a time. Part of him went tight with dread at the possibility the police might soon have evidence linking Dan Foster's murdered wife to the attempts on Ellie's life. Another part of him hoped they'd make the connection and he could convince Ellie to get the hell out of Dodge.

If he couldn't, those handcuffs were sounding better and better.

Grabbing the mooring line, Jack leaped onto the barge. It rocked under his weight and earned him a frown from the plainclothes detective and a grunt from Eric Chapman. The kid spread his legs wider to brace himself and held the detector steady over the water.

"It's showing a depth of seven and a half feet," he informed the wet-suited diver beside him.

"The water's only a little over six feet deep at this point," Ellie told Jack in an aside. "That means the bullet's burrowed into the mud."

A uniformed officer propped his elbow on the barge railing to add support for the heavy detector Eric held suspended over the river. Discoverer Two pinged noisily as the diver opened the air valve on his tanks, wrapped his lips around his mouthpiece and pulled down his face mask. Black fins waving, he went over the side with and hit with a splash. He glanced up to take a bead on the wand and dove straight down.

Shoulder-to-shoulder, Jack and Ellie peered over the railing. Mud swirled to cloud the green water. Air bubbles bobbed to the surface. The muted pops when they broke sounded so much like the silenced shot Jack had head last night that his palms got slick with sweat where they gripped the rail.

Dragging his gaze from the swirling water, he scanned the scene. He spotted Cyrene, seemingly relaxed and at ease as she sipped a frothy pink drink at a patio restaurant and let her glance drift over the gawking onlookers. Mackenzie was on the steps, dividing her attention between the voice in her head and the drama being played out before her.

Despite the added security, tension wrapped Jack in a tight coil. Scarface was out there. In one of the high-rise hotels overlooking the river. Lounging at a table in one of the restaurants. Mingling with the crowd. Watching. Waiting.

Jack could feel the killer. Smell him. He just couldn't see him. He edged closer to Ellie, angling his body to shield hers. His nerves were stretched so tight the whoosh of the diver breaking the surface damned near had him flinging her facedown in the barge.

Muddied green water streamed over the diver's mask. Spitting out his mouthpiece, he shoved his mask back on his head with one hand and held up the other.

''Is this what we're looking for?''

The expended shell gleamed in the sunlight. Unlike the artifacts Ellie and her team had recovered from the archeological site, the copper casing was clean and new and bright.

"It's a forty-one hollow point," Ellie confirmed with a single glance.

"Same caliber as the bullet that killed Joanna Foster," Detective Harris muttered.

Flashing Jack a quick glance, he dug a plastic evidence bag out of his pocket. In their first meeting, the SAPD veteran hadn't tried to disguise his cynicism about harebrained professors who stirred up more controversy than they could handle. He was coming around. Fast.

"We'll run it through ballistics ASAP," he promised Jack. "Should have a comparison between it and the bullet that killed Mrs. Foster by late this afternoon. Tomorrow at the latest."

Jack grunted, not happy with the prospect of another day's wait. Ellie didn't much like it, either. Frowning, she glanced at her watch.

"It's just a little past noon. I need to go out to the dig. I don't want to waste the rest of the day."

"Sorry. Consider it wasted."

"I'll go on out," Chapman volunteered.

After unstrapping the heavy mental detector, the young grad student swiped the sweat from his brow with a freckled forearm. The sight of the gleaming copper shell casing had sobered him…and turned him into a reluctant ally.

"Carstairs is right, Ellie. You shouldn't make yourself any more of a target than you already are."

Her mouth pursed. Jack was all set to ask Detective Harris for the loan of his handcuffs when she caved.

"All right. Tell the rest of the folks I'm sorry for leaving wrap-up operations to them. We'll convene in my room at 8:00 p.m. for a team meeting. In the meantime, I'll go through yesterday's field notes and start working on the draft report."

That was the plan, anyway. She returned to her suite, took a quick shower to wash away the sweat and stink of stirred-up river water. After a quick sandwich ordered from room service, she settled in front of her laptop and attacked the field notes, but the constant comings and goings of Jack's associates played havoc with her concentration.

With her fascination for all things electronic and near genius with computers, Mackenzie Blair was certainly an interesting study. Particularly after her sudden and rather startling transition from techno-geek to femme fatale. The calm, tranquil woman Jack referred to as Cyrene proved every bit as compelling in her quiet way.

Ellie caught only snatches of their discussion of cover points and team surveillance of Mackenzie's upcoming meeting with Dan Foster. She couldn't miss, however, Blair's rueful grin when she reported the gist of her conversation with someone named Lightning.

"You were right," she told Jack. "He had a few choice words to say about me tagging Foster."

"No kidding."

"He also reminded me I'm not—" She caught herself, threw a quick glance at Ellie and obviously modified whatever she'd intended to say. "I'm not one of you field jocks. I'm to take every possible precaution."

At that point, Ellie felt impelled to intervene. Abandoning any pretense of working on her report, she swung around in her chair.

"You don't have to do this, Mackenzie. I'm the one Foster and his hired gun may be after. You shouldn't put yourself in danger."

"Hey, don't spoil my fun. I don't get the chance to come out to play with the big guys all that often." She checked her watch. "I'd better go start getting beautiful. It could take a while."

Ellie said nothing more until Blair and the woman named Claire departed. Her eyes thoughtful, she waited for the door to click shut behind them before voicing the question hovering in her mind.

"Who are those people, Jack? For that matter, who are you?"

He took his time responding. Folding his arms, he leaned his hips against the back of the sofa. "Who do you think I am?"

"Obviously not a small-time bodyguard in need of work."

Flushing a bit at the memory of how she'd insisted

her uncle hire him, believing he might need the income, she left her chair.

"So tell me. Who are you? What do you do for a living?"

"Does it really matter, Ellie?"

The question took her back nine years. She could almost hear the echo of her fierce arguments, see Jack's stony face.

"No," she said softly. "What you do for a living *doesn't* matter. It never did."

Jack took the hit without blinking. He deserved it. More than deserved it. Considering the discussion over, she started to turn.

He caught her with a hand on her arm. Drawing her closer, he curled a knuckle under her chin.

"I'm not saying I was wrong all those years ago, you understand?"

"What are you saying?"

Bending, he brushed her lips with a kiss so gentle Ellie almost melted on the spot. When he raised his head, his expression was so serious her stomach did a little flip.

"This isn't the time or the place for promises," he said, his tone gruff. "Not with everything that's coming down on you right now. But if anyone walks away this time, Elena Maria, it'll have to be you."

Chapter 10

Ellie was still thinking about Jack's *non* promise when her team arrived from the dig. They'd shut down operations early. For good, this time.

"The deputy director of the park service called," Sam Pierce related, his craggy face both resigned and regretful. "He asked for you. I gave him your cell phone number and the number here at the hotel, but he said I could relay the message."

"Let me guess. NPS has pulled our funding."

Pierce nodded. "They left just enough in the kitty to restore the site."

She'd sensed it was coming. Given the pressure exerted by the Texas congressional delegation, the park service could hardly do anything else if they hoped to fund future projects. Still, the abrupt termination stung. Fighting a crushing sense of disappointment, Ellie listened while the others briefed her.

"We packed up all the equipment," Orin Weaver advised. "Eric loaded your van. I've got mine loaded and ready to go. I'll give you my input for the final report tonight and head home tomorrow."

The forensic anthropologist had other jobs waiting, Ellie knew. He was a frequent consultant for local, state and federal law enforcement, and his services were in demand. She couldn't ask him to stay and work gratis.

"Thanks, Orin." Forcing a smile, Ellie shook his hand. "I appreciate all you've contributed to this project."

Dr. Dawes-Hamilton wasn't quite as ready to abandon ship. "I've got some grant money back at Baylor waiting to be spent," she told Ellie. "I'll press ahead with the authentication process on the artifacts we've shipped to the university and send you a copy of my findings."

If the archeologist could use her department's grant money to authenticate the rifle and scraps of clothing found with the remains, Ellie could certainly scrape together enough funds to pay for DNA testing. Assuming, of course, the donors were still willing to provide samples.

"You'll have to decide what you want done with the bits and pieces we recovered in the past couple of days," Sam Pierce said. "I imaged and catalogued them on the computer, but most of the stuff is just junk."

The bits and pieces he referred to filled a large cardboard box. At Ellie's request, Eric lugged it in and deposited it beside her computer.

"Nothing there the park service might want to add to their collection of items found in and around Mission San Jose?" she asked Sam.

"Nope."

"I'll go through the box one more time. Maybe the archdiocese of San Antonio will be interested. Or the Alamo's museum director."

"Maybe," Sam said doubtfully.

"If not, I'll dispose of the unwanted items when I make arrangements for the site restoration."

Which would take her all of a day or two.

Ellie bit back a sigh. The project she'd begun with such enthusiasm and intellectual curiosity had generated nothing but controversy and was about to ignominiously fizzle out. Adding insult to injury, someone apparently wanted to fizzle *her* out with it.

Well, she hadn't completely finished with this project yet. Or with Mr. Dan Foster and his shadowy, frightening associate.

When she indicated as much to Jack and *his* team some time later, however, he flatly vetoed her suggestion that she slow roll the cleanup and shutdown operations in an attempt to draw out the killer.

"No way! You're out of here as soon as you pack up and hit the road."

"What good does it do to leave? Scarface could easily waylay me on the road or follow me home."

"You're not going home."

"Oh?"

She threw a glance at Mackenzie and the woman they called Cyrene. Both returned it with absolutely blank expressions. Obviously, this was Jack's show. They'd take their cue from him.

"All right," she said, swinging back to the man in charge. "I'll bite. Where am I going?"

"You're taking a nice long vacation at an undisclosed location."

"Don't be ridiculous. I can't just disappear indefinitely. I've got a house, a job, students who've signed up for courses that begin in less than a month."

"They can sign up for other courses. Until we bring Scarface down, I don't want you in his line of fire."

"I hesitate to point out the obvious, but I'm *already* in his line of fire. Where I'll stay until, as you say, you bring the bastard down. Seems to me you have more chance of accomplishing that right here. It's just a matter of flushing him out of hiding."

"Yeah, right. With you as bait."

Deliberately, Ellie suppressed the queasy feeling in her stomach. She was no coward, but neither was she a fool.

"Look, I'm not proposing to stroll around town with a target pinned to my back. I'm merely suggesting we turn the termination of the dig to our advantage. We can leak rumors that I'm drafting my final report. Set up a press conference. Hint that I'm going to distribute vivid images of my research and visits to the Alamo along with copies of the report. Make Foster and his hired killer sweat and, hopefully, provoke them into doing something stupid."

"It's too risky. I won't let you stake yourself out like a sacrificial goat for a cold-blooded killer. Nor do I think it's wise to reignite the anger of every hotheaded Texan who thinks you're messing with history."

Mackenzie broke her silence. "Ellie doesn't have to actually release the report to the media. All we need to do is make Foster *think* the release is imminent. I can help there."

Jack shot her an evil look, but before he could nix the plan that seemed to be forming despite his objections, Cyrene broke ranks, as well.

"When she meets with Foster tonight, Mackenzie could also let drop something about the bullet recovered from the river," Claire said in her quiet voice. "The possibility that the police might make the connection between the attacks on Ellie and his wife's murder would add significantly to Foster's stress levels.''

"The doc's right," Mackenzie argued. "I could spin all kinds of rumors. Really put Foster in a real puddle of sweat. My bet is he'll dump me like radioactive waste and head straight for the nearest phone to contact his hit man."

"Yeah," Jack snarled. "That's my bet, too."

In the face of his fierce opposition, Mackenzie backed off. Ellie, however, held her ground.

"I guess I'm taking my cue from William Barrett Travis. I'm drawing a line in the sand. I'll take my stand here, in the shadow of the Alamo."

"Right! And just look where that got Travis. Depending on how your final report reads, he either went down on the walls or was shot in the back of the head while trying to escape."

Jack regretted the scathing retort the moment it left his lips. The color leached from Ellie's cheeks. Fear flickered in her brown eyes for a moment before she resolutely quashed it. Holding his gaze, she summoned a shaky smile.

"I'm not running—or walking—away."

Jack's head jerked up. Her message came through loud and clear. To him, at least.

The other two in the room sensed the sudden charge in the air. The women exchanged questioning glances, but neither said anything until Renegade conceded with a bad-tempered growl.

"All right. We'll play this out a little while longer. Mac, see what you can stir up tonight. First, though, I'd better advise Lightning on the change of plans."

Jack had a feeling Nick Jensen wasn't going to be happy with the latest turn of events. Not only was the niece of Mexico's president offering herself up as bait for a killer, Mackenzie Blair was making an inch-by-inch transition from chief of communications to fully engaged field operative.

Jack was right.

Lightning was *not* happy.

He'd made a call to the President to bring him up to speed on the situation in San Antonio, then advised Colonel Luis Esteban, as well.

As afternoon wore into evening, Nick reminded himself that his chief of communications had gone through much of the same training as OMEGA's field agents. All headquarters personnel took marksmanship training, endured the water, jungle and desert survival courses and learned hand-to-hand combat from experts to give them an appreciation of what operatives went through in the field.

With the added benefit of her Navy background, Nick knew his comm chief could more than hold her own in just about any environment. But the gold Mont Blanc pen Maggie Sinclair had given him tapped an erratic beat as he leaned back in the leather captain's chair just past eight Washington time.

"You're not wearing a ring." Dan Foster's disembodied voice floated through the Control Center. "Does that mean you're not married?"

Nick's pen took another bounce. Foster was about as subtle as one of his eighty-ton earthmovers.

Eyes narrowed, Nick studied the scene Cyrene was beaming to the headquarters via the pen-size camera in her purse. The wall screen displayed a detailed portrait of dim lighting, gleaming wood and the couple in the booth.

The builder had hooked an arm around the back of the booth. His white shirt was unbuttoned at the top to accommodate his bull-like neck. Gold glinted on his wrist. Pure, unadulterated male lust gleamed in his eyes.

Nick could understand why. Mackenzie hadn't opted for subtle, either. If she drew in too deep a breath, she'd fall right out of that dress.

"Isn't my marital status irrelevant to this discussion?" Her husky little laugh rippled through the control center like warm velvet. "We're here to talk business."

"I make it a point to learn everything I can about the people I do business with," Foster countered with a predatory grin. "It gives me a leg up in negotiations."

"We haven't entered into negotiations."

"We might. We just might. So what's the story? Are you married, engaged or otherwise involved?"

"At the moment, none of the above. And I'd better warn you, I'm *very* ticklish in that particular spot."

Nick's pen went still.

Mackenzie waited until the builder had brought his left hand from under the table and clasped it loosely around his drink before picking up the conversational ball.

"What about you? Are you married?"

"I was. My wife died a few months ago."

"A few months ago?" With a slight turn of her head, Mackenzie let her glance drift to the arm draped around her shoulders. "I'd offer my condolences, but you seem to have recovered from your loss remarkably well."

"Joanna and I had what you might call a mutually satisfactory arrangement rather than a marriage. She didn't ask any questions. Neither did I."

"How did she die?"

"She was kidnapped and murdered."

"Good God! How awful for her. For you, too."

"Yeah, it *was* pretty awful." Making a show of pain, Foster knocked back the rest of his drink. "I still have nightmares."

Nick just bet he did. No doubt those nightmares had started about the time reports about Elena Maria Alazar's work in and around the Alamo hit the front pages.

Tucking his pen in the pocket of his camel sport coat, he leaned forward. Cyrene was providing backup for Mackenzie, leaving Renegade to guard Elena. Nick would have trusted either operative with his life. He couldn't seem to get past the fact that Mackenzie was trusting them with hers.

Grimacing, Nick remembered the strip he'd ripped off Jack for crossing the line with Ellie. Nick had better take a dose of his own medicine. Personal and professional didn't mix in this job.

"Like any big city, San Antonio seems to have a lot of murders," Mackenzie commented. "A woman staying at my hotel was shot at just yesterday. Right on the Riverwalk."

"That so?"

With apparent disinterest, Foster signaled to the waitress to bring another round of drinks. Settling against the booth, he stroked his fingers over his companion's bare shoulder.

"I heard about it from the concierge," she continued with a theatrical little shudder. "According to him, police divers recovered the spent shell casing."

Foster's hand froze.

"I have to admit, he didn't seem all that surprised that someone had taken a shot at this woman," Mackenzie confided ingenuously. "Evidently she's been stirring up all kinds of trouble. Something to do with the Alamo. Supposedly the story made all the papers. Maybe you read it?"

"No."

"Really? Well, you might see something soon.

Rumor is the woman's about to release some bomb-shell report.''

Careful, Nick thought. *Go careful here.*

''The concierge says she's reserved the hotel's ballroom for a big bash,'' Mackenzie continued air-ily. ''She's going to give some kind of multimedia presentation, complete with sound, light and digital images.''

Having neatly dropped her own bombshell, she snuggled into the crook of Foster's arm.

''Now, about the presentation *I'd* like to give you on the communications for your building. If you'll tell your secretary to provide me a set of blueprints, I can work up a detailed plan.''

''Yeah, I'll do that.'' Disengaging, Foster reached into his back pocket and dragged out his billfold. ''Listen, I'm sorry to run out on you like this, but I just remembered something I have to do.''

''Now?''

''Now.''

Tossing a bill onto the table, he started to slide out of the booth. Mackenzie halted him by the simple expedient of hooking a hand in his belt buckle.

''I want this contract.'' Her voice dropped to a seductive purr. ''I'm fully prepared to give you a special deal.''

Foster's startled glance dropped to his belt. What-ever Mackenzie's hand was doing behind the metal buckle had snagged his serious attention. Beads of sweat popped out on the man's brow. Nick felt a few pop out on his own.

"How long are you going to be in town?" the builder asked, his voice hoarse.

"That depends on you."

"I'll call you, okay?" He patted his shirt pocket. "I've still got your card. You see my secretary, tell her I said to make you a copy of the blueprints. Tomorrow, the next day, we'll, uh, get down to business."

With a smile that hovered between a pout and a promise, Mackenzie released him. Foster slid out and disappeared from the screen.

A moment later, Mackenzie winked at the camera. Her amused voice floated through the speakers.

"He might lose my business card, but until he changes belts, he'd not going to lose the bug I just stuck to his buckle. Over to you, control."

A half hour later, the team assembled in Jack's suite.

He and Ellie had listened via satellite link to the exchange between Mackenzie and Foster. Together with Mac and Cyrene, they now waited for the builder to take care of the something he'd suddenly remembered he had to do.

Foster made the call from his home just after 9:00 p.m. Shaking her head, Mackenzie adjusted the volume on the receiver.

"What a jerk!"

Amazed that the man would be so stupid as to risk calling from his home, she listened to the muted beeps of the dial tone. Although muffled, they were picked up by the bug she'd planted on Foster. The control center's computers would translate those beeps instantly into numbers.

"Yeah?"

"This is Foster. Things are happening. Things I don't like. You have to take care of that business we discussed. Like, now."

"I'm workin' it."

"Work harder!"

The phone was slammed down.

The four people in the hotel suite maintained their silence, hoping for something more. An indiscreet mutter. A short, angry tirade. Anything that might give them a better clue as to Foster's arrangements with his contract killer. All they got was the clink of glass on glass and the sudden blare of the TV.

"Well, Scarface didn't say much," Mackenzie told the others, "but we should be able to get a voice print out of it. Let's see if Control got a lock on the number Foster dialed."

Jack stood at her shoulder. His face darkened as he read aloud the message that flashed on her screen.

"The number was traced to the call notes for a cell phone registered to Harold Berger, 2224 River Drive, Austin."

Cyrene's silver blond brows lifted. "The dead man?"

Nodding, Jack cut a quick glance at Ellie before turning to Mackenzie.

"Can you work a satellite lock on the transmissions to and from that cell phone?"

"Not unless we catch a call during a broadband sweep of the entire transmission area. The chances of that range from zero to minus zero."

Jack didn't like the answer. He could see that Ellie didn't much care for it, either.

"Control will take it from here," Mackenzie advised, shutting down her unit. "If there's any further contact tonight, they'll let us know."

She rose, as did Cyrene. The psychologist cocked her head, studying Jack's grim face.

"You're tired. I'll take first watch."

"I'm okay."

"You need sleep."

"I'm okay."

"I won't let anything happen to her," Claire said gently. "I promise. And you'll be right here, a shout away."

Jack knew damned well he was operating on sheer nerves. He also knew that he wasn't about to let Ellie out of his sight tonight. Or any other night, if he had any say in the matter.

"You stand first watch here in my room," he suggested by way of compromise. "Ellie can leave the connecting door open. I'll bed down on the couch in her sitting room.''

Cyrene accepted the altered arrangements without argument. While she went to her room to collect a few things, Jack grabbed a pillow and blanket from the closet and deposited them on the rolled-arm sofa in the living room. He'd pulled out his automatic to check the magazine before he noticed the woman standing in the shadows. Hugging her arms, she stared blindly at the curtained windows.

''Ellie?''

She jumped and swung to face him. Her eyes were wide, their pupils dark pools.

''You okay?''

A shiver rippled down her spine. She didn't answer for a moment. She couldn't. The fact that she'd just heard Foster issuing her death warrant had taken some time to sink in, but sunk it had. She understood how the Alamo's defenders must have felt when Santa Anna delivered his final warning that he'd give no quarter if they continued their hopeless resistance.

Panic swept through her. She came within a breath of telling Jack that she'd changed her mind, that she wanted out of the hotel, out of the city and as far away from the Alamo as he could take her.

But she couldn't erase the mental image of that line in the sand. As much as she wanted to, she couldn't bring herself to tuck tail and run.

"I'm okay. Just a little shivery. Guess I've got the air-conditioning turned up too high."

The lie was so obvious Jack didn't bother to challenge it. Instead, he crossed the room, caught her in his arms and returned to the sofa. The cushions whooshed under his weight as he wedged his back into the corner. Settling Ellie comfortably in his lap, he gave her his warmth.

This wasn't the moment to tell her he'd also given her his heart. Not when Cyrene was moving about in the next room within easy earshot and a killer lurked somewhere in the shadows. He'd come as close to it as he dared earlier, when he told her she'd have to be the one to walk this time. She'd answered obliquely but unmistakably. That would do. For now.

Propping his chin on Ellie's head, he began to murmur the repetitive, hypnotic mantras that would ease the tension locking them both in steel cages.

For the first time in longer than he could remember, the relaxation techniques didn't work. Jack couldn't blank out the shape and scent of the woman nestled against him. Couldn't empty his mind of how near he'd come to losing her.

Again.

He didn't realize his hold had tightened around her until she squirmed and tipped her head back.

"Jack?"

Her eyes held a question, but it was her mouth he ached to answer. The tendons in his neck corded with the effort of holding back. He'd compromised her safety once by losing himself in her arms. He was damned if he'd do it again.

"Sorry," he murmured, loosening his hold. "Try to relax."

Lowering her head to his shoulder, she wiggled into a comfortable position. The movement of her bottom drove every mantra Jack had learned over the years right out of his head.

Gritting his teeth, he focused all his psychic energy on maintaining control over his body. He might not ever walk upright again after tonight, but he would keep Ellie safe at all costs.

Chapter 11

Detective Harris contacted Jack just after ten the next morning.

"We ran the bullet retrieved from the river through ballistics and sent the results to the FBI, who worked the Foster kidnapping and murder. You were right. The same gun fired both."

Jack's stomach clenched. No question now. Their conjectures had moved right out of the realm of possibility and into cold, lethal reality.

"So where does that leave us?"

"With some very excited FBI field agents who want to know just how the heck you tagged Dan Foster. They'd like to meet with both of us this afternoon. Two o'clock. Their offices are in the courthouse at 615 East Houston Street. Can you make it?"

His glance went to Ellie. She sat at the desk, a cold cup of coffee beside her. She was in jeans and a short-sleeved white shirt, its tails tucked in neatly at her trim waist. Dark circles shadowed her eyes, but her face wore a look of intense concentration.

She'd been hard at work since breakfast. Jack suspected her fierce attention to detail sprang as much from a need to keep her mind off her stalker as from a determination to tie up every loose end on her project. From the stack of field notes sitting beside the computer, he suspected she'd be at it for hours to come.

"Yes," he told Harris. "I can make it."

Cyrene would provide security for Ellie. Jack would take Mackenzie. She'd made the initial connection between Foster and Scarface and run it through her contact at the FBI. She'd also had two face-to-face sessions with Foster. The FBI guys were going to want to hear about those. And about the tag she'd put on the builder.

Mackenzie would know how to finesse that bit of electronic eavesdropping. OMEGA took its direction directly from the President and wasn't bound by the same rules and restrictions when it came to field operations as other government agencies, but it didn't hurt to head off jurisdictional disputes at the pass.

Cyrene was one of OMEGA's best. Jack could trust her to keep Ellie safe. Still, he had to force himself to the door after lunch.

With Jack gone, the suite seemed emptier, the afternoon endless.

Cyrene curled up on the sofa with a spy novel. Ellie made calls to several companies for estimates to fill in the excavation site. She also called each of the volunteers, thanking them for their assistance at the dig before putting the final touches on her report.

As she scrolled through the pages, she fought another sharp stab of disappointment. She and her team had come so close to fitting the pieces of the puzzle together. She hated to end the project by offering supposition and conjecture instead of fact.

Setting aside her personal feelings, she forced herself to take a critical eye to the report. She'd fine-tuned the sections detailing the discovery of the remains, the assembly of the team, the recovery of artifacts and the on-site authentication processes the team had employed. She'd add Dr. Dawes-Hamilton's laboratory results later.

The section dealing with the remains was the hardest to work on. She'd already incorporated Dr. Weaver's anthromorphical analysis, which included the basic physical features as extrapolated from the skeletal characteristics.

Male. Caucasian. Average height for his time. Age thirty to thirty-five. Indications of incipient arthritis, with some degree of bone degeneration in joints.

Propping her chin on her hands, Ellie stared at the terse summary. The shadowy figure of a Tejano formed in her mind. He didn't wear buckskins and rough frontier garb as depicted by Hollywood in its movies about the Alamo, but a broadcloth suit such as a doctor or lawyer might have donned. His face was shaded by a wide brimmed-hat to protect it from the fierce Texas sun. He grasped a double-barrel shotgun in one hand.

Who are you? she wondered for the hundredth time. *Did you escape the Alamo? If so, when? Before the final assault or after?*

Blowing out a long breath, she hit the laptop's keys.

By three o'clock the walls were starting to close in on her. Abandoning the computer, she decided to attack the cardboard box Sam Pierce had deposited on the floor. It took all her concentration to remain focused on the objects she pulled out to examine and verify against the inventory.

None of them appeared to hold any real historical significance. A broken snaffle bit. Several coins. A rusted tin plate. What looked like a piece of a plowshare.

At the bottom of the box, she found the dented silver disc Jack had turned up during his stint with Discoverer Two. Evidently the National Park Service hadn't considered the item worth salvaging. It was tarnished almost black, pitted all the way through and not anywhere near as valuable as the solid silver bracelet circling Ellie's wrist.

She'd never given Jack anything in return, she realized. She'd never had the opportunity. She'd only seen him once after he slipped the two-inch band on her wrist, and that was when she'd stormed into to the U.S. Embassy compound to engage in a furious, one-sided argument with a certain hardheaded Marine.

The small, dented concho wasn't in the same class as the expensive bracelet, but polished, it might make a keepsake for Jack. Something to remind him of these days in San Antonio—as if either one of them would need reminding!

Fingering the disk, she dialed housekeeping. "This is Dr. Alazar in Room two ten. Would you please send up a small jar of silver polish and a soft cloth? Yes, silver polish. Thanks."

Claire looked up from her book, her glance curious.

"Jack found this out at the site," Ellie explained, displaying the bit of silver. "I'm going to clean it up for him as a souvenir."

A maid delivered the requested items. No doubt the Menger's management was wondering just what Dr. Alazar was up to now. After passing the woman a generous tip, Ellie went to work on the concho.

Gradually, the tarnish disappeared to display an intricate pattern stamped into the silver. The design was extraordinarily artistic, with scrolls and swirls and a tiny oak leaf cut in the center. The oak leaf wasn't a traditional Mexican symbol. It struck her as more like a design a silversmith would do for one of the Tejanos.

A vague memory stirred in the back of her mind. She'd seen a design like this before. She was sure of it. But where?

Puzzled, she took it to the desk. A search of her database turned up no images that matched it. Only after a second lengthy search did she remember the design stamped into the silver work on the shotgun she'd photographed at the Alamo.

A touch of the old excitement fluttered in her veins. Pulling up the image of the double-barreled shotgun, she examined the elaborate scrollwork on the sidings and butt plate.

Yes! There it was! A small oak leaf in the center of the scrollwork.

Her excitement taking wing, she pulled up images of the gun they'd found some yards away from the skeletal remains. The silver was still tarnished, the design difficult to decipher, but Ellie could swear it was the same.

Okay. All right. What did she have here? Not a whole lot, except the possibility that the smith who worked the silver facings on both guns might very well have crafted the concho Jack had found.

Once more she attacked the computerized files.

The minutes ticked by. Undaunted, Ellie conducted search after search before she found a reference to Josiah Kennett, one of the Alamo's more obscure defenders. Or more specifically, to the silver conchos on Josiah's Kennett's hat.

Suddenly, Ellie remembered the miniature portrait of an unsmiling young man, his collar tight around his neck and his face shadowed by the wide-brimmed hat favored by Mexicans and Tejanos alike. She'd seen his miniature in the Alamo, right next to the man's tattered Bible.

The thrill she always felt when the pieces of a historical puzzle began to fall together gripped her. Closing her fingers over the silver disk, she swung around in her chair.

"When's Jack going to be back?" she asked Claire.

"I don't know. Soon, I would think. Why?"

"I need to make a quick visit to the Alamo. I think I may have a clue to the identity of the remains that my team and I recovered. I won't know until I get a shot of a portrait in the museum and enlarge it."

"It's not a good idea for you to leave the hotel," Claire countered gently. "Not until Jack gets back, anyway."

Ellie had no intention of taking a step outside the Menger without Jack. "Can you contact him? Find out where he is?"

"Of course."

Slipping a small cell phone out of her pocket, she pressed a single button.

"This is a secure instrument," she said with a smile as she put the instrument to her ear. "Mackenzie would take it as a personal insult if anyone ever eavesdropped on one of us."

Like Mackenzie herself was doing to Dan Foster. Recalling the builder's terse call last night, Ellie almost changed her mind about leaving the confines of her hotel room. A cowardly little voice inside her head whispered at her to hunker down behind strong barricades and stay there until it was safe to come out.

She couldn't cower behind drawn shades and closed doors forever, though. And a determined foe could breech even the strongest walls...as the defenders of the Alamo had learned all too well.

Shoving her hands in her pocket, she listened to Claire's side of the conversation with Jack. Evidently, she'd caught him and Mackenzie on their way back to the hotel. His first instinct was to flatly veto Ellie's request for a quick trip next door. His second, to acknowledge the bitter truth. If two OMEGA agents backed-up by their chief of communications couldn't keep her safe, no one could. Period. End of story.

"He'll meet us in the lobby in fifteen minutes," Claire advised. "Hang loose while I run a check of the halls and the elevators."

Her movements graceful and unhurried, she hooked her purse over her shoulder and exited the suite. In her gray pleated linen slacks, narrow belt and sliky green blouse, she could easily pass for one of the hotel's well-heeled guests instead of a highly specialized protective agent.

At least that's what Ellie assumed she was. One of these days, she vowed, she'd have to pin these people down on exactly who they worked for. Pacing the room, she rubbed her thumb over the silver disk and waited in mounting impatience for Claire's return.

"All clear," she advised after a short absence.

Snatching up her camera and a curled-brim crushable straw hat, Ellie hurried out the door.

Jack and Mackenzie met them as they stepped out of the elevator. He didn't have much to say about his visit to the FBI and Ellie knew better than to probe for details in such a public place. He did, however, want to know what the hell was behind the urgent visit to the Alamo.

"This."

Pulling her hand out of her pocket, Ellie uncurled her fingers. "It's the concho you found at the excavation site. Look at the design. I've seen it before, Jack. I'm sure I have. I just need to verify where."

He shook his head but could tell from the suppressed excitement in her voice that she thought she was on to something.

"Okay. Just stay with me, and do exactly what I say the instant I say it. Cyrene, you take point. Mac, you've got rearguard."

With Claire strolling ahead and Mackenzie trailing behind, they walked outside. After the controlled chill of the hotel's air-conditioning, the muggy Texas summer hit them like a baseball bat. Hastily, Ellie slipped on sunglasses and tugged her hat lower on her brow to shield her face. Her skin began to dew before they covered half the distance to the monument next door.

The usual crowd milled around Alamo Plaza, snapping photos in from of the mission and slurping up ice-cream cones purchased from near-by vendors. The hair on the back of Ellie's neck prickled as her glance roamed over the tourists. Was Scarface lurking among these camera-laden sightseers?

Her pulse skittered when she caught a glimpse of a straw Stetson similar the one the killer had been wearing when she'd unintentionally photographed him with Dan Foster, but the face beneath the brim belonged to a short, stocky man of Hispanic descent. He carried a baby in one arm and had looped the other around his young son's shoulders.

Blowing out a sigh of relief, Ellie pushed through the door set in the massive walls. Once inside, a welcome wash of cool air surrounded them.

"Oh-oh!"

Elle's murmured exclamation put Jack on instant

alert. Claire's head whipped around. Her hand disappeared inside her purse. Mackenzie hurried up to
add to the living shield around Ellie.

"Do we have a problem?" Jack asked softly.

"Yes," Ellie whispered, "but not the one you're
worried about. See that docent?"

All three agents eyed the gray-haired volunteer
cheerfully passing out brochures.

"If she recognizes me," Ellie whispered, sliding
her sunglasses back up the bridge of her nose, "she'll
call out the palace guard. Would one of you distract
her long enough for me to slip by?"

Claire had no difficulty claiming the docent's attention. A simple question about the age of the wood
beams overhead had the volunteer craning her neck
to point out original iron nails and peg-joints. Ellie
kept her face averted and whisked right past.

Once inside the courtyard, the ripple of excitement
she'd felt earlier in her hotel room returned. History
was both her profession and her passion. Solving the
mystery of the remains found in a creek bed five
miles south of the Alamo might not rank up there
with discovering the Dead Sea scrolls or deciphering
the Rosetta Stone, but putting a name to the man who
died alone and unmourned would afford her immense
personal satisfaction. Consequently, she paced in a
fever of impatience until Claire re-joined them.

"The exhibit I want to see is in that long, low
building."

Cyrene, you stay outside and surveil the crowd,"
Jack instructed, slipping a hand under Ellie's elbow.
"Mac, I want you at the entrance."

Nodding, both women took up their posts.

As she and Jack entered the Long Barracks, Ellie
kept a wary eye out for Dr. Smith. The museum director had insisted she submit written requests for
further access to the private collections. He hadn't
said anything about the public exhibits, but she
wasn't taking any chances.

The display case containing Josiah Kennett's tattered Bible and miniature was in a small room filled
with artifacts belonging to the Alamo's lesser-known
defenders. Ellie's gaze shot straight to the hat shad-
ing Kennett's young, unsmiling face.

A narrow leather strap banded the crown. Ellie's
breath caught as she noted the silver conchos orna-
menting the band. Given the small size of the portrait, she couldn't tell whether or not the design included a small oak leaf.

A quick glance around the room showed she and
Jack were alone. A clutch of tourists peered at exhibits in the room across the hall, but for the moment
at least, Ellie had Josiah Kennett all to herself.

"I just need a few pictures," she said, excitement
simmering in her veins.

She was reaching her digital camera when Jack's
cell phone gave a discreet ping. Sliding it out of her
pocket, he glanced at the digital display.

"It's Mac."

Flipping open the phone, he tried to acknowledge the call. A frown creased his forehead. The static coming through the line was so loud even Ellie could hear it.

"Something's breaking up my transmission," Jack muttered. His gaze snagged on the intrusion detection device mounted above the exhibit cases. "Probably the infrared beams from those security alarms."

"Probably," Ellie agreed, absorbed by the contents of the exhibit case. "The Alamo is more wired than Fort Knox."

Jack glanced down the way they'd come. The halls were clear. The rest of the tourists had moved onto another section of the museum. Mac was right outside, ten steps away. Jack could keep Ellie in sight while he checked with Comm on the transmission problems.

"Do not leave this room," he ordered tersely. "I'll be right back."

He took two steps down the hall. Caught a faint whisper of sound. Sheer instinct spun him down and around.

There was a soft pop. A fiery explosion of pain. With a small grunt, Jack took the bullet.

Unaware of the lethal drama taking place just paces away, Ellie fiddled with the settings for her camera and snapped away. She'd have to do more research on Kennett. Verify where he came from.

How he ended up at the Alamo. If possible, determine what weapons he was carrying when he joined
the ranks of defenders.

Humming, she zoomed in on the miniature. Only
then did the significance of the small leather pouch
slung over Kennett's left shoulder sink in. On closer
examination, she decided it could well be a courier's
pouch, like those carried by army scouts. Identical,
in fact, to one she'd seen in a portrait of James Allen,
the sixteen-year-old courier who carried Travis's last,
desperate appeal for reinforcements out of the Alamo
on March 5th, the day before Santa Anna attacked in
full force.

She knew from historical documents that Travis
had sent out a number of couriers, some identified
by name, some not. James Butler Bonham, a lawyer
and fellow South Carolinian from Travis' home
county, had tracked down Colonel James Fannin at
Goliad. Captain Juan Seguin carried an appeal directly to Sam Houston. Young James Allen made
that last, hopeless ride.

As she tried to recall references to the other, un-
named couriers, the possibilities burst like fireworks
in Ellie's mind. Maybe Travis had gleaned intelligence warning of the imminent attack. Maybe he'd
worried one courier might not get through enemy
lines. Maybe he'd sent two, sacrificing badly needed
firepower in the hope that one of them would make

it. Maybe young Kennett wasn't fleeing the massacre on March 6th, but trying urgently to prevent it.

She'd have to go back through the inventory of artifacts recovered at the dig. Check to see if there was any bit of metal or scrap of rotted rawhide that might have come from a pouch. Snapping away, she recorded several more digital images. The creak of a floorboard behind her had her whirling to share the exciting possibilities with Claire and Jack.

It wasn't Jack who stood in the doorway, however. Or Claire. It was a tourist in mirrored sunglasses and a black ball cap emblazoned with NYPD in gold letters. Ellie took in the reassuring lettering and started to smile a welcome. Her smile turned into a sick gulp when she noticed the white scar tracing a path in the tanned folds of the man's neck.

"Hello, Dr. Alazar."

She didn't need the faint mockery in his greeting—or the long, lethal silencer screwed to the muzzle of the pistol in his hand—to know she'd come face-to-face with her stalker.

"Jack!"

Her frantic scream bounced off the thick walls.

"Your friend can't hear you," Scarface said with a grim smile. "He can't hear anything."

Despair knifed into Ellie, so sharp and lancing she almost doubled over.

"No!" she moaned. "Dear God, no!"

"Yes," the thug taunted. "And now…"

"You bastard!"

Acting from sheer animal instinct, Ellie reached behind her and smashed her digital camera into the glass exhibit case. Before the first, shrieking alarm had filled the air, she brought her arm forward and flung her camera at Scarface.

What was left of the glass exhibit case behind her shattered. Ellie didn't hear the gunshot over the screaming alarm, didn't even care that his first shot had missed. Fingers curled into claws, she launched herself at the man.

She had to get past him, had to get to Jack....

Before she reached him, there was a bright flash. An unseen force propelled her attacker into the room. He collided with Ellie, took her down. Frantic, she tried to scramble out from under his dead weight.

"Ellie!"

The hoarse croak came from above her. A fist reached down, yanked at the weight crushing her into the floor. The instant she could wiggle free, she rolled onto all fours. Broken glass cut into her hands and knees. The alarm shrieked like the hounds of hell, but Ellie felt nothing, heard nothing but a roaring rush of joy.

Jack! It was Jack! Blood flowered like a bright, obscene hibiscus on his shirt. His face was dead white. But his eyes were feral as he went down on one knee beside her, keeping his weapon trained on the man sprawled in a growing puddle of blood the whole time.

"Were you hit?"

She saw his mouth move. Saw, too, the near panic in his eyes as they raked her from head to foot.

"What?"

Mackenzie raced into the room at that moment, followed a second later by Claire. Ellie saw the weapon in their hands, saw their lips moving, but couldn't hear anything over the deafening clang.

Jack motioned to Claire to keep Scarface covered and whirled back to Ellie. "Where were you hit?"

She shook her head, unable to hear but grasping the reason for his fear. Blood splattered her white blouse and drenched her jeans from the knees down.

"I'm okay!" she yelled. "But you…" Frantic, she fluttered her sliced palms at blood-drenched shirt. "You've been shot!"

The alarm cut off abruptly. Her ears ringing, Ellie tried to understand what Jack was saying as he gently grasped her wrists.

"It looks worse than it is. Damned bullet ricocheted off the bone and took me down for a few moments, but it went clear through."

Mackenzie's sneakers crunched on the glass as she crouched down beside them. "Just hold still," she instructed, "we'll get you patched up and…"

The sound of running footsteps cut her off. Jack chopped a hand in the air, motioning her to one side, and shoved Ellie behind him. Claire slammed her shoulder blades against the wall, where she could keep both Scarface and the door covered. Ellie tensed for another attack.

Dr. Smith burst in. His jaw dropping, the pudgy museum curator gaped in disbelief at the carnage. His wild gaze flew from the unconscious figure on the floor to Claire, to Jack. Finally, to Ellie.

Red suffused his cheeks. His eyes bugged behind his glasses. He sputtered, choked, spit out Ellie's name like a curse.

"Dr. Alazar! I should have known! What in God's name are you doing?"

The combination of stark terror and relief so deep and sharp it ate like acid into her bones had her snapping right back.

"What does it look like we're doing, you twit? We're fighting the second battle of the Alamo."

Chapter 12

Keeping a tight lid on the shoot-out at the Alamo required the combination of Renegade's forceful personality and Lightning's political influence. There was no way they wanted Foster to know his hit man had gone down. Not yet anyway.

Dr. Smith went tight-lipped with indignation and disapproval when informed that the President's special envoy had placed a call to the head of the Daughters of the Texas Revolution. She had agreed that this unfortunate attack on the niece of the President of Mexico was a matter for the police, not the press.

The various law enforcement agencies involved

concurred. Wheeling Scarface out of the Alamo on a gurney, they informed the gawking tourists that there had been an accident. He died in the ambulance on the way to the hospital without recovering consciousness. His demise left a frustrated Detective Harris and two very disgruntled FBI agents with no clue to the hit man's real identity. Or with anything linking him to Daniel Foster except Ellie's photograph.

"Which," Claire said later that evening in Ellie's hotel suite, "Foster's lawyers will argue is merely a chance juxtaposition of two visitors to a popular historic landmark."

"Yeah, right," Mackenzie groused. "Some visitors."

She took a turn around the sitting room, hands shoved into the front pockets of her jeans. Her Nikes left tracked imprints on the plush carpet. The sex kitten who'd nestled up to Foster at the bar last night was gone. In her place was a woman imbued with a sense of purpose.

"We all know Foster hired that bastard to off his wife. We just can't prove it. There's no record of money transfers from his bank to suspicious accounts. No traceable phones calls besides the one we intercepted, and that was made to a cell phone we *think* belonged to Scarface but can't locate, as he didn't have it on him when he died."

Ellie sat quietly in an armchair, her bandaged hands tucked loosely around her waist. More bandages showed beneath the hem of her shorts, padding her knees. She couldn't get quite as worked up as Mackenzie over Daniel Foster's probable guilt. Not just yet. She was still recovering from the trauma of dodging the assassin's bullet.

Jack had remained quiet since they'd returned from the emergency room, too. As he assured her, the bullet had merely glanced off his clavicle. Luckily, the bone hadn't shattered. The entrance and exit wound were clear. He'd refused pain pills and now listened to the others with every evidence of attention, but his glance shifted to Ellie at frequent intervals, as if to make sure she wasn't about to keel over from blood loss or delayed shock.

"Foster's got to be a mass of raw nerves right now," Mackenzie continued. "He'll be expecting a call from Scarface with confirmation he's done the deed. Every hour that goes by without word is going to torque up the pressure on Danny Boy. Sooner or later, he's going to do something stupid. I say we make it sooner."

"I say we let him sweat," Jack countered. "For tonight, anyway."

"Yes, but—"

"I agree with Renegade," Claire said, rising from her chair with fluid grace. "As long as the incident at the Alamo doesn't leak to the press, Foster will think Scarface is still on the hunt. That puts the advantage squarely in our court. Let's use the time to think through our next moves.''

Hooking an arm through Mackenzie's, Cyrene gently but firmly steered the younger woman out. Jack followed them to the door, shot the dead bolt and armed the intrusion detection alarm he'd rigged when he'd arrived. The immediate threat to Ellie had been eliminated, but he couldn't shake an edgy sense of incompleteness. She still had to wrap up the last details of her project. He still had to decide whether to go after Foster or leave him to the locals.

Then there was the small matter of where he and Ellie went from here.

Tonight wasn't the time to talk about it, though. His wound hurt like hell and Ellie looked ready to drop. Her shoulders drooped. Fatigue left shadows like bruises under her eyes. If that weren't enough to rouse Jack's fiercely protective instincts, the bandages on her hands and knees would have done the trick.

"You should get some sleep," he said, his voice gruff with concern. "You've had a hell of a day."

"It was rather eventful." A faint smile feathered her lips. "Do you think Dr. Smith will ever let me set foot inside the Alamo again?"

"I'd say you'll have to do some real sweet talking first."

"Maybe he'll relent when he hears my theory about young Josiah Kennett."

"Maybe. In the meantime, I suggest you forget Smith, forget Kennett, forget the second battle of the Alamo and crawl into bed."

"I might, if you crawl in with me."

Her smile deepened, starting an ache almost as fierce as the one in Jack' shoulder.

The docs said you should rest," she reminded him, using her bandaged hands to lever herself awkwardly out of her chair. "Let's go to bed."

Yeah, right. As if he'd get any rest lying next to Ellie. Particularly when she stopped beside the bed and lifted her hands helplessly.

"You'll have to undress me. I can't work my shirt buttons with these bandages."

Jack's throat went dry. "I think I can manage that."

"I think you can, too."

His blood was pounding, but he kept his touch gentle as he unbuttoned the linen camp shirt Claire had helped her into after returning from the E.R.

The docs had assured Jack they'd extracted all the glass shards from Ellie's palms and knees, and that the cuts weren't deep enough to require stitches. Yet the gauzy bandages were a grim reminder as he eased the shirt down past her elbows.

If he hadn't caught that faint whisper of sound and dodged the assassin's bullet, if Ellie hadn't won a few precious seconds by flinging her camera at the killer, she might have been the one wheeled out of the Alamo on a gurney. The thought made his chest squeeze so tight he couldn't breathe.

She didn't seem to notice the sudden constriction in his breathing. Heeling off her shoes, she kicked them aside and waited patiently for Jack to start on her shorts.

By the time he'd stripped her down to her bra and bikini briefs, more than just his chest was tight. Hard and aching, he skimmed a knuckle down the hollow of her belly.

"You sure you don't want another of the pain pills the docs prescribed?"

"I'm not feeling any pain at the moment. My sleep shirt is over there, on the chair."

Jack retrieved the scrap of cotton. The damned thing had put in him a sweat the first time he'd seen her in it. He was feeling pretty much the same effect now. Ignoring the painful pull in his shoulder, he eased it over her head.

"Now you," she murmured.

Ellie's throat closed as he eased off his shirt. The neat bandage wrapped around his shoulder brought

the afternoon's horror rushing back. Inching sideways on the bed, she made room for him.

"Fine pair we are," he said with a wry grin.
"Come here."

Slipping his uninjured arm under her, he brought
her closer. Ellie cradled her head in his good shoulder. Her palm rested on his chest. Beneath her fingers
was the strong, sure beat of his heart.

"This afternoon," she whispered, "when Scarface
said you couldn't hear my scream. I thought…I
thought I'd lost you."

"I thought the same thing when I barreled through
the door and saw you go down."

Curling a knuckle under her chin, he tipped her
head up. His eyes held hers.

"A few nights ago, you asked if I'd ever loved
you. I've never stopped, Ellie."

"Oh, Jack!" She wanted to weep with the joy and
the sharp, stinging regret. "We wasted so many
years. So many days and nights we could have
shared."

"I know." His thumb brushed her cheek. "I don't
plan to waste any more."

She hooked a brow. His teeth flashed in a rueful
grin.

"After tonight," he amended. "Go to sleep,
sweetheart."

The bright bubble of joy was still with Ellie the

next morning, when she bundled into one of the hotel's plush terry-cloth robes, made a futile attempt at wielding a hairbrush, and ambled into the sitting room in search of Jack and coffee.

She found both, as well as two other men. One was a stranger. The other Ellie recognized immediately.

"Colonel Esteban!"

"Elena. It is good to see you again."

Moving with the grace of a jungle panther, he came forward and bowed over her hand. Ellie had met him on several occasions during her visits to her aunt and uncle, yet even her awareness of the shadowy world the colonel worked in couldn't blunt the impact of his dark eyes, luxuriant mustache and Caesar Romero smile. Ellie might have fallen in love with Jack Carstairs all over again, but she wasn't blind. Nor was she oblivious to the tension in the air.

Frowning, she threw a quick, questioning look at Jack. He had obviously rolled out of bed well before she did. Showered and shaved, he filled a cup with black coffee and carefully passed it into her bandaged hands.

"How's your shoulder?" she asked.

"Hurting but healing. How are your hands?"

"The same."

Downing a grateful sip, Ellie returned her attention

to the colonel. "It's good to see you, too. What are you doing in San Antonio?"

"Your uncle sent me. He was informed of the unfortunate incident at the Alamo and wishes to be assured you took no serious hurt."

"I'm fine."

The colonel's glance drifted to the white gauze.

"I just took a few cuts and bruises," Ellie said. "Really. You can tell Uncle Eduardo I'm up and walking and ready to get back to work."

"Perhaps you should tell him yourself. He would like you to come stay in Mexico until the U.S. authorities take care of this bastard who wants you dead."

"We were discussing that last night. Getting hard evidence against Daniel Foster could take months, even years. I can't—correction, I *won't*—run away and hide that long."

The stranger had said nothing, but her protest brought him forward. He was a tall man, dressed with casual elegance in knife-pleated gray slacks and an Italian knit sport shirt.

"We don't believe it will take as long as that, Dr. Alazar."

"And 'we' are?"

"Sorry. I should have introduced myself sooner. I'm Nick Jensen, special envoy to the President of the United States."

Ellie had spent enough summers with her uncle to have a good grasp of the various levels of bureaucracy inherent in any government. Despite that background, she didn't have a clue what a special envoy did.

Jensen didn't enlighten her. "Like your uncle, the President is concerned for your safety. That's one of the reasons we sent Renegade—Jack—to protect you."

"You sent him? But I thought—that is..."

"That your uncle hired him? Let's just say it was arranged through my office."

Well, she'd already figured out Jack Carstairs wasn't the down-at-heels gumshoe she'd first thought him, but the fact that he worked for the special envoy to the President of the United States took some getting used to. Struggling with the mental readjustment, she picked up on Jensen's comment.

"You said concern for my safety was one of the reasons you sent Jack to San Antonio. What were the others?"

"Quite frankly, the President also worried that the ill will displayed toward you could erupt into ugly anti-Mexico sentiments, possibly derail the North American Free Trade Association Treaty. Neither Mexico nor the United States wanted to see that happen."

A sick feeling curled in Ellie's stomach. She didn't look at Jack. She couldn't.

"Let me get this straight," she said slowly, the coffee cup cradled in both hands. "You—all of you—got involved in this mess because political issues were at play?"

"Political issues are always at play," Jensen said, "but your safety was the overriding concern, of course."

His rueful smile might have charmed Ellie under any other circumstances. At the moment, she was too numbed by the thought that she'd been a political pawn in a game she'd known nothing about.

"Of course," she echoed dully.

"It's still the overriding concern," Jensen continued smoothly. "Foster has already demonstrated the lengths he'll go to. He hired one killer. There's nothing to say he wouldn't hire another. The President thinks you should consider your uncle's offer. Or at least let us take you to a safe house until Jack and the others put Foster on ice."

"I see."

Carefully, she placed the cup on the sofa table. She felt frowsy and frumpy and at a distinct disadvantage facing Esteban and Jensen in her bare feet and bathrobe. But those feelings paled beside the ache that formed around her heart when she turned and saw Jack's face. There was no sign of the tender lover in his stony expression. No spark of warmth in his cool blue eyes.

"What do you think? Should I leave San Antonio?"

"Yes."

She waited for some softening of the hardness in his face, some indication another separation would rip him apart as much as it would her. When he didn't so much as blink, Ellie's hurt took a sharp right turn into anger.

No! Not again! Jack Carstairs had gone all stubborn and tight-jawed and noble about what was best for her nine years ago. No way in *hell* she was going to let him do it again!

Her spine snapped straight. Matching him stare for stony stare, she made her position ice clear. "You said I'd have to be the one to walk away this time. I told you then and I'm telling you again, I'm not walking. So you can just deal with it. All three of you!"

On that note, she exited the scene. Slamming the bedroom door behind her was childish and unnecessary, but it gave Ellie intense satisfaction.

The thud reverberated through the sitting room. Esteban and Jensen stared at the closed door for some moments before turning to Jack.

"You were right," Nick conceded with a grin.

"She didn't take kindly to the idea of being hustled out of town. We'll have to fall back and regroup."

Luis Esteban wasn't quite as ready to admit defeat. Smoothing a palm over his lustrous black hair, he gave the closed door a disgruntled glance. "You must speak with her, Carstairs. Convince her to leave. You and I, together we will handle this Foster."

"You and I?"

"President Alazar has suggested I remain in San Antonio to, ah, provide whatever assistance you might require."

Hell! That's all Jack needed! A watchdog hired by Ellie's uncle looking over his shoulder, second-guessing his every move. The urge to tell the colonel just what he and Eduardo Alazar could do with their so-called assistance rose hot and swift in Jack's throat.

He swallowed the words, right along with his pride. With Ellie still at risk, he wasn't about to turn away any help. Lightning made the bitter pill easier to take when Jack had assembled Comm and Cyrene in his suite some fifteen minutes later.

"Luis Esteban worked a hairy mission with Maggie Sinclair some years ago," he said by way of introduction. "She and Thunder both came to my office to meet with him a few weeks ago. The colonel's gone into the private sector now, but he's still one of us.''

That was all the endorsement Mackenzie required. ''Anyone Chameleon considers a good guy *is* a good guy in my book.''

Her unconditional acceptance won her a quick, slashing grin from Esteban. Those gleaming white teeth and glinting black eyes sent the gulp of coffee she'd just taken down the wrong pipe. Choking, Mackenzie rattled the cup onto the table, splashing lukewarm liquid on the polished surface.

Claire was more reserved in her reaction to the newcomer. Reaching across to pound her sputtering colleague on the back, she gave the colonel a cool, assessing look.

Esteban's gaze was considerably warmer. Where in God's name did OMEGA recruit these women? Maggie Sinclair was in a class by herself. The one called Mackenzie possessed a lively animation and a quick wit. But this one, this mature, composed beauty, stirred his blood in a way no woman had since... Well, since Maggie Sinclair.

He'd have to find out more about her. His resources might not reach as deep or as far as OMEGA's, but he could still access information when he wanted it.

''So why are you and the colonel here?'' the dark-haired Mackenzie asked Lightning when her fit of coughing subsided. "What's the plan?"

"The plan is, ah, under review at the moment. As to what Colonel Esteban and I are doing here... We flew down to convince Dr. Alazar she shouldn't take any more risks."

"Well, darn!" A look of acute disappointment crossed Mackenzie's expressive face. "I wish I'd been here to hear Ellie's response to that."

Even Cyrene was amused. "Renegade made the same argument. Apparently you two didn't have any more success than he did."

"We'll try again," the colonel assured her. "She must realize we have only her best interests at heart."

Her best interests.

The words clanged like a klaxon in Jack's head. He'd uttered them himself. More than once. For the first time, he recognized how pompous and patronizing they must sound to Ellie. As if she weren't intelligent or rational or mature enough to recognize her needs.

He still wanted her out of San Antonio. His overriding instinct was to shield her, to safeguard her from all harm. If anything, the shoot-out at the Alamo yesterday had reinforced the edgy feeling that she wouldn't be out of danger until they nailed Foster.

Jack had finally learned his lesson, though. He couldn't make her decisions for her. Nor could anyone else. It was time he acknowledged that fact. Past time.

"Why don't we get Ellie's input into the revised plan?"

The suggestion earned him a frown from Esteban, a curious glance from Lightning and an emphatic second from Mackenzie. Claire sent her approval in the form of a small nod.

Crossing the room, Jack rapped on the bedroom door. "Ellie? We want to talk to you."

The door swung open. She emerged from the bedroom wearing crisp linen slacks, a sleeveless turquoise top and a decided air of authority.

"I have a few things to say to you, too." She made a quick sweep of the room, nodding at Claire and Mackenzie. "Good, you're here. I won't have to repeat myself."

Moving to the center of the sitting room, she tucked her injured hands under her crossed arms.

"All right, listen up. Here's what we're going to do. I'm going to finish my research into Josiah Kennett and coordinate the final report with my team. That should take twenty-four hours, less if I get right to it. Then I'll release the team's findings. Right here, in San Antonio. We'll gather the public forum Mackenzie hinted to Foster about and blow it up big.

Invite the media. The mayor. The city council. Influential members of the business community and country club set. Including," she announced grimly, "one Dan Foster."

"Oh, this is good," Mackenzie breathed. "Really good! Danny Boy will go ballistic when he gets the invite."

"We'll hold the reception here at the hotel," Ellie continued, directing her comments to the three men, daring them to object. "It's short notice, but we have to hope they can accommodate us. I'll work the crowd at the reception. I'll also contrive to get Foster alone at some point. You," she said, pinning Jack with a look that could have cut glass, "will come up with some scheme to get him to incriminate himself."

"I think I can manage that," he drawled.

"Good!" With the air of one who's firmly in charge, she surveyed the group. "Does anyone have any questions or comments?"

"Just one," Nick said in the short silence that followed.

Ellie braced herself for an argument. To her surprise, Jack stepped between her and the President's special envoy.

"We're doing this her way, Nick."

His firm, no-arguments tone had Ellie blinking. A few moments ago, he'd stated flatly that he wanted her out of San Antonio. She still hadn't quite recovered from the hurt of knowing he'd been following a political as well as a personal agenda all this time.

Now he was not only acknowledging her right to make her own decisions, it sounded as though he was fully prepared to sacrifice a second career for her. Thoroughly confused, she couldn't decide whether to whoop in delight or warn him to back off, fast.

Not that he would have listened. From the set to his jaw, it was obvious Jack had no intention of backing down.

"Ellie's had her baptism under fire," he told Jensen. "She's earned her spurs. We're doing this her way or not at all."

Once again, she was surprised. Instead of taking offense, Jensen merely nodded.

"You're in charge on this mission, Renegade. You call the shots. I was simply going to offer my restaurant as an alternative site for the big announcement. It will hold as many or more than the hotel's ballroom and give us better control over security."

Ellie blinked. "You own a restaurant?"

"Actually, I own several."

"Try several dozen," Mackenzie muttered. "Ever hear of Nick's?"

"Good heavens, yes! There's one in Mexico City. In Acapulco, too, I think."

Mackenzie held up a hand and ticked off a few

others. "And Paris and Rome and Hong Kong, New York, Vegas, Palm Springs. You'll find a Nick's about everywhere the rich and famous gather."

"And none of them," he commented with a glinting look in her direction, "serve sausage, double pepperoni and jalapeño pizza."

"Too bad." She tossed the words back. "You won't get my business unless you diversify your menu."

"We'll have to talk about that. Along with the expanded operation role you've assumed on this mission."

"Uh-oh." Mackenzie's brows waggled. "This doesn't sound good."

"Let's go to my room, shall we? I had Mrs. Wells book one just in case I decided to stay." He gave the others a polite nod. "If you'll excuse us."

With the exaggerated air of a martyr about to meet her fate, Mackenzie preceded him to the door.

Chapter 13

Mrs. Wells hadn't just booked Lightning a room. She'd reserved the presidential suite.

Of course.

The palatial five-room suite took up most of the top floor and gave stunning views of the Alamo. Ornate furnishings from a bygone era made Mackenzie feel as though she'd stepped into the bustling days of Texas before the turn of the century, when cattle was king and Judge Roy Bean's Lillie Langtry thrilled audiences from coast to coast. The massive antique sideboard that housed a bar and entertainment center had been carved from some dark, brooding wood. So had the canopied four-poster she glimpsed in the bedroom. The thing looked like it could comfortably sleep six!

"Forget the ballroom and your restaurant," Mackenzie commented. "You could fit the mayor, the city council, the entire country club set and every news crew in Texas in this suite."

"Let's talk about a certain member of that country club set." Tossing his room key onto the sideboard, Nick leaned his hips against it and slid his hands in the pockets of his gray slacks. "You got pretty chummy with Foster at the bar the other night."

Airily she waved a hand. "All part of the job, chief."

"But not part of your job. When I instructed you to put a tag on the man, I didn't say to do it yourself."

"You didn't say not to, either."

"Don't play games with me, Comm."

The whip in his voice brought her snapping to attention. "No, *sir!* I would never do that, *sir!*"

Nick eyed her for long moments. The coins in his pocket clinked as he jiggled them in one hand.

"Did any of your Navy commanders ever consider a court-martial?"

"One or two." Grinning, she abandoned her exaggerated pose. "I was usually shipped out before matters reached that point."

"I may just ship you out this time, too."

"That's your option," she agreed breezily, refusing to admit this annoyed, unsmiling Nick was just a little bit intimidating. "But I was thinking our friend Foster might want a date for the big do. Someone who can give him an alibi when his hired gun shows up at the party.''

''Why would he think Scarface will show?''

''Well, I sorta figured I'd tell him.''

Lightning's eyes narrowed. The coins clinked again. Mackenzie held her breath until he broke the small silence.

''How?''

She was on her turf now. Confident, eager, she sketched her idea.

''We got a voiceprint on Scarface when Foster called him. It's not much. Only a few words. But we can digitize the sounds and run them through a phonetics databank, then use a synthesizer to imitate his exact intonation. Tweety Bird could chirp into the phone, and Foster would think it was his hired killer.''

He didn't argue her skills. No one could. When it came to electronics, she was the best.

''Think about it, chief. Foster will want to attend the function to make sure the hit goes down *before* Ellie makes her announcement and releases her report to the media. But he'll need an alibi, someone who can swear he was otherwise engaged when it happens. I'll be that alibi. I'll also make sure we get our boy on tape when Renegade figures out how to get him to incriminate himself.''

Lightning wasn't convinced. ''There's a good

chance Foster already paid for one death and is working on a second. I don't like the idea of my chief of
communications turning up number three on his
list.''

''Aww. Are you worried about me, boss?''

''Worrying about OMEGA's operatives comes
with the title of director, Blair, but you're adding a
new dimension to the mix.''

Mackenzie would have had all four incisors
yanked without the benefit of anesthetic before she
admitted to the thrill his sardonic reply gave her.
Still, she couldn't hold back a smug little smile as
she sashayed to the door.

''I'll get my folks at headquarters to work running
the voiceprint through the phonetics database.''

While Jack accompanied Nick to his San Antonio
bistro to perform an initial security assessment, Ellie
got to work. Her bandaged hands made things awkward, but she spent several hours engaged in a flurry
of phone calls and e-mail exchanges with universi-
ties, libraries and genealogists. Finally, she tracked
down the clerk of Kearnes County, Texas, where Josiah Kennett's family had reportedly homesteaded.
After a hand search of county records, the clerk located an eighty-seven-year-old great-great grand-
daughter of Kennett's only sister.

Ellie got Dorinda Johnson's number from information. To her delight, the woman who identified

herself as Dorrie answered the phone. She sounded frail but had no difficulty grasping Ellie's background and interest in the tumultuous events of 1836.

"I remember my great-granddad telling us about the Runaway Scrape," she said in a wavery, paper-thin voice. "That Generalissimo Santa Anna you mentioned came up with a plan to move foreign settlers to the interior, replace them with Mexicans and cut off all immigration. Said he was going to execute every foreigner who resisted. After the Alamo and the massacre at Goliad, I guess the American settlers round these parts figured he meant business. Every one of 'em, including my great-great-granddaddy, abandoned their land and skeedaddled over the border to Louisiana."

If Ellie remembered correctly, the frantic scramble labeled the Runaway Scrape took place in early April, a month after the Alamo fell and just weeks after Colonel James Fannin and his force of four hundred Texians surrendered to Santa Anna. Under the mistaken impression they would simply be expelled from Mexico, the Tejanos were marched back to Goliad, where Santa Anna had them summarily shot.

Word of the massacre spread across Texas like prairie fire. Frightened settlers loaded everything they could into wagons and rushed helter-skelter for the U.S. border. Soldiers in Sam Houston's ragtag army abandoned ranks in droves to assist their fleeing families. Houston was left with only a little over nine hundred volunteers to face Santa Anna's well trained, well equipped and—until then—victorious army.

"Great-granddaddy said his grandpa's cabin was burned to the ground," Dorrie related, "but he came back and rebuilt after Houston beat the pants off Santa Anna at San Jacinto."

"Did your great-grandfather ever mention a great-uncle named Josiah Kennett?"

"Seems like he did, but I don't recall much about him, 'cept he died at the Alamo."

"Are you sure?"

"Well, that's what we were always told. I've got some old family pictures and letters stashed in a trunk up in the attic. I think there's one in there that talks about Josiah. Might take me a while to get to it, though. Doc says this new hip of mine isn't ready for stairs yet."

"That's all right!" Ellie said hastily. "Please don't go up to the attic."

She did some quick thinking. Kearnes County was less than an hour's drive from San Antonio. She could get out there and back by late afternoon.

"Would you mind if I drove out to your place and took a look through that trunk?"

"You come right ahead, missy. I'd enjoy the company."

Snatching up a pen, Ellie jotted down directions to her place. "Thanks. I'll be there by two-thirty or so."

Trying to contain her excitement, she filled the time until Jack's return by negotiating a contract for the site restoration and drawing up a list of invitees for the reception.

Mackenzie pounded on her door just before noon, every bit as excited and even more impatient for Jack and Nick's return. They arrived at the Menger a while later. Ellie wasn't quite sure how the colonel had managed to become a permanent member of their little group, but the others seemed to have accepted his presence.

Plugging a microphone into a small gray box, Mackenzie claimed their immediate attention.

"Wait till you hear this."

Her eyes gleaming, she spoke a few phrases into the microphone. The synthesizer translated the words into a deep rasp. The result sounded so much like the man who'd attacked Ellie in the exhibit room that goose bumps raised on her arms.

When the raspy echo faded, Mackenzie looked across the mike at Ellie. "You're the only one of us who heard him live. What do you think?"

"I think it's amazing. And just a bit scary."

"Good!" Her glance went to Jack. "Want to make the call to Foster?"

"Let's work out the wording, then you can go for it."

A few minutes later, Mackenzie dialed Foster's

private number. When an answering machine clicked on, she rasped out a brief message.

"Word on the street is our friend plans to release her report tomorrow night. I'll be there to make sure it doesn't happen."

Ellie knew it was a ploy. She was standing right there, had watched Mackenzie mouth the words. Yet the threat sounded so ominous that she had to work to match Mackenzie's smug grin when she cut the connection.

"There! That'll up Foster's pucker factor. I'll wait till he gets his invitation to the soiree to make the next call."

Recalled to her part in the drama, Ellie produced the list she'd worked on earlier. "Believe it or not, I convinced Dr. Smith to help me pull it together. The man's so eager to see me leave town—and so relieved that it looks like I'm not going to rewrite the history of his Alamo—that he actually volunteered the names of the high rollers who've contributed to the Alamo Restoration and Maintenance Fund."

She met Jack's glance.

"Foster's wife was one of the contributors."

A savage satisfaction glittered in his eyes. "That gives us the perfect rationale for including the bastard among the invitees. Think you can notify everyone on the list today?" he asked Mackenzie.

"Consider it done. I'll zap the list to my people

at headquarters. Given the short notice, they'll have to fax the invites. We'll make sure it looks as though they came from Dr. Alazar. As soon as they're out, I'll put in another call to Foster and offer myself as his date. Then,'' she announced, "I'm going shopping."

Jack hooked a brow. "Again?"

"Again. The results of my last expedition seemed to impress Danny Boy. This time, I'll pull out all the stops and knock him off his feet. Literally."

"No, you won't."

Jack's reply came hard and fast, preempting Nick's.

"Foster's mine. All mine. No one knocks him off his feet but me."

Faced with his vocal opposition and Nick's tight frown, Mackenzie backpedaled. "Okay, okay. He's all yours. But I still need to go shopping. I didn't bring anything suitable for a black-tie affair. How about you, Claire? Ellie?"

The psychologist's gaze drifted around the small group. It didn't linger on Luis Esteban for more than an instant, but whatever she saw in his face caused her to incline her head in a graceful nod.

"I'll join you."

"Ellie?"

"I can't make it this afternoon. I want to drive down to visit a fourth-generation relative of one of the Alamo defenders."

The excitement she'd felt at the start of her project seeped into her veins. Her face eager, she turned to Jack.

"She lives in Kearnes County, less than an hour from San Antonio. She thinks she has some letters in her attic that contain information about Kennett. I'm also hoping I can talk her into providing a DNA sample. Will you go with me?"

The first real smile she'd seen in days crept into his eyes. "Try going anywhere without me."

The trip through the South Texas countryside was just what Ellie needed. After the stress of the past weeks and the sheer terror of the attack in the Alamo, the wide-open plains rolled by with soothing monotony.

Jack was at the wheel of the rented Cherokee. His eyes shielded behind mirrored sunglasses, he kept a close watch on the rearview mirror. They weren't followed this time. Nor did they engage in any high-speed chases. Gradually, even Jack relaxed.

They drove south on 181 for some forty miles, roughly paralleling the course of the San Antonio River as it meandered to the Gulf. Just past Hobson, they turned onto a two-lane county road that ran straight as an arrow between fields fenced by barbed wire. Ellie consulted the directions she'd scribbled down earlier.

"Dorrie said her place was three point four miles down this road."

Nodding, Jack took a fix on the odometer. Three point four miles later, a dented mailbox atop a weathered post proclaimed the Johnson place.

A dirt track led to the house, perched on a slight rise a quarter mile from the road. The Cherokee jounced over deep ruts. Dust swirled in a long plume behind, announcing their arrival long before they drove over a cattle guard and pulled into the yard.

The original structure must have been constructed in the early Texas dogtrot style, with separate sleeping, cooking and eating quarters on either side of a walk-through breezeway. Native stone walls enclosed the original sections, but succeeding generations had tacked on clapboard additions and enclosed the breezcway.

Leaning heavily on a walker, Dorrie Johnson hobbled out to greet them. Shaded by the tin roof that extended over the front porch, she was a tiny figure in a bright yellow blouse, denim jumper and sturdy sneakers. To Ellie's consternation, she'd prepared a small feast for her visitors.

"My molasses cookies won first prize at the county fair for near onto three decades," she announced smugly. Her walker thumping, she led Jack and Ellie into the front parlor and waved at them to have a seat. "The pecan crop wasn't all that good last year, though, so I baked up a sweet potato pie, too.''

Jack didn't appear to find any fault with the pecans. He consumed a plateful of cookies, washing them down with sweetened iced tea, before tackling a hearty sampling of pie. Ellie was too enthralled by the memories Dorrie shared of her family to do more than nibble at the rich sweets.

''Salathiel Charles Kennett and his bride homesteaded this place in twenty-eight. Hauled everything they owned west in a covered wagon. Like I told you, they left in a hurry in thirty-six.''

At Jack's questioning look, Ellie explained the Runaway Scrape.

''They came back, though,'' Dorrie continued complacently. ''One of their offspring or another's been squatting on this patch of dirt ever since.''

''Do you know where Salathiel hailed from?''

''He was from Alabama. Barbour County, best I recall. His wife was from Sparta, South Carolina. Dorinda. Dorinda McLaren. Want to guess who I was named for?''

Ellie jerked upright in her seat. Ignoring the playful question she fired one of her own.

''Your kin came from Sparta?''

Dorrie's eyes twinkled. ''Didn't I just say so, missy? I'll admit I'm getting a mite forgetful these days, but I can pretty well remember the words that just popped out of my mouth.''

"Yes, of course. I'm sorry. It's just that… Well, William Barrett Travis, the commander of the troops at the Alamo, moved to Texas from Sparta, South Carolina, too."

"You don't say!"

Carefully placing her iced tea on a coaster, Ellie scooted to the edge of her seat.

"Historical documents indicate Travis arrived at the Alamo armed with a double-barreled shotgun, among other weapons. There's one on display up there in San Antonio bearing a mark that traces to a gunsmith in Sparta. I found another buried in a creek bed some miles south of the city with the same mark. We're trying to determine who that gun belonged to."

"Don't know that I can help you there, missy. Seems I remember great-granddaddy talkin' about a shotgun *his* daddy carried west with him. Could have been made by that gunsmith you're talking about, but I don't know what happened to it."

"Could he have given it to his brother, Josiah, to take with him when he joined the Texas Army?"

"I 'spose so."

"Maybe there's something in those letters you told me about that will give us more information," Ellie hinted.

"Maybe," Dorrie said doubtfully. "You're welcome to crawl up to the attic and take a look."

The tin roof trapped the heat and held it under the eaves. Dust motes danced and swirled in the hazy light cast by the bulb dangling at the end of a long cord.

Switching on the flashlight Dorrie had provided for extra illumination, Ellie stepped over bundles of old *National Geographic*s and stacks of yellowed sheet music. A zigzagging course through the treasured junk of several generations took her to the steamer trunk pushed under the eaves. Leather peeled in strips from its sides and humped top. The rusted hasps were sprung and hung uselessly on their hinges. Grunting, Jack used his good arm and worked it out far enough for Ellie to raise the lid.

She gasped in delight. He swiped at a trickle of sweat and groaned.

"It's going to take hours to go through all this stuff."

"It might take you hours," she retorted, the historian in her affronted by his lack of faith in her abilities. "I know what I'm looking for. Just pull up that crate, get comfortable and hold the flashlight steady."

Jack did as ordered. Hunkering on the sturdy crate, he planted his elbows on his knees and aimed the beam of light at the yellowed letters, old newspaper clippings and faded family photos.

Her still tender knees made kneeling impossible, so Ellie sat cross-legged beside the trunk. Despite the bulky bandages on her hands, or maybe because of them, she handled the clippings and documents with extreme care. She skimmed each with a keen eye before setting it aside. Inch by inch, the stack beside her grew.

Jack found the woman digging through the trunk far more intriguing than its contents. She probably didn't have any idea how beautiful she looked to him at this moment. Dust swirled around her. Sweat glistened on her forehead and upper lip. White streaked her hair where she'd caught a cobweb. She was totally absorbed by those yellowed scraps of paper, as thrilled by the past as Jack was nervous about the future.

He'd dropped enough hints. Hell, he'd come right out and admitted that he'd never been able to get her out of his head or his heart. He'd had to work to say the words. He'd never told any woman he loved her, Ellie included.

He was pretty sure she loved him, too. She'd told him flat out she wasn't wasn't walking away from him. And she certainly held nothing back the night she'd flamed in his arms. Yet Jack wanted to hear the words. Needed to hear the words.

"Ellie."

"Hmm?"

"Last night…"

She glanced up then, curiosity warring with impatience to get back to the letter in her hand.

"What about last night?"

"I meant what I said. I've never stopped loving you."

The words hung on the suffocating air. Chewing on her lower lip, Ellie considered his quiet declaration.

"Last night," she said after a long moment, "I believed you. For a moment this morning, I had my doubts."

"I know. I saw the hurt in your eyes when Lightning brought up that business about the treaty. You have to know politics have nothing to do with what's between us."

"To quote your friend Lightning, political issues are always in play. They certainly were nine years ago."

"But not this time. Marry me, Ellie."

"What?"

"You said it yourself. We've wasted too many days and nights already. Marry me. Here in Texas, or in New Mexico or wherever we can get a license with the least hassle and delay."

Helplessly, Ellie gaped at him. Sweat trickled down his temples. With the flashlight's beam backlighting his face, he looked like a character from a B-grade horror flick. She couldn't believe the man had chosen this hot, musty attic to ask for the commitment she'd ached to give him nine years ago, but she wasn't going to argue the time or the place. As she'd told Jack, she knew her mind then and she knew it now.

"Yes," she said simply. "I'll marry you. Whenever and wherever you want."

With a small, inarticulate sound, he bent to seal the agreement. The kiss left them both breathless and several degrees hotter than before.

"Better finish with that trunk," he warned with a crooked grin, "or Miss Dorinda might hear some strange thumps coming from her attic."

Chapter 14

Ellie found the prize she'd been searching for near the bottom of the trunk, tucked inside an old Bible. The yellowed, folded sheet had torn at the creases and almost came apart in her hands. Carefully lifting the bottom edge, she took one look at the signature and gulped.

"Here." Her hands clumsy and trembling in their gauze wrappings, she passed the letter to Jack. "I don't want to take a chance on tearing this further. Unfold it, will you, and hold it so I can read it."

Trading the letter for the flashlight, he lifted the folds and tilted the letter toward the beam. Ellie came up on her knees without so much as a blink at the pain and leaned on Jack's thigh. Her heart thumping, she peered at the spidery script.

March 5th
1836
Elijah—

I don't have time for more than a few lines. The colonel's sending me & another out shortly. God willing, one of us will make it through & bring back reinforcements. If there are none to be had, I'll rejoin my company here at the Alamo.

Ammunition's running low, but I still have enough for pa's short-barrel to give a good accounting. She fires as true as the colonel's. Guess she should, seeing as the same smith cast both.

They're calling for me now. I'll leave this letter with the captain's wife, as many of the company are doing. She's promised to see them delivered if she survives the attack we all know is coming.

Yr brother,
Josiah Kennett
Private
Texas Volunteers

Ellie's throat ached at the letter's simple poignancy. The satisfaction of knowing she'd found the last vital piece of the puzzle didn't begin to compare with the admiration she felt for Kennett's courage and sense of duty.

"James Allen made it to Goliad," she murmured, leaning against Jack's knee, "but Fannin delayed sending troops until it was too late. I wonder where Josiah was headed."

"Guess we'll never know." Carefully, he folded the letter. "Do you think Dorrie will agree to contribute this to the collection at the Alamo?"

"I hope so!"

Dorrie not only agreed to let Ellie take the letter, she also cheerfully provided a DNA sample. After rolling a cotton swab around in her mouth, she stared at the tip for a moment before dropping it into a plastic baggie.

"You sure that's all you need?"

"If that doesn't do it, we know where to find you."

Ignoring Ellie's protests, Dorrie thumped out to the porch to see them off. "Y'all come back any time."

"You promise to bake more of these and we will," Jack said, carrying the bag of molasses cookies the older woman had pressed on him with the same care Ellie carried her bagged letter and DNA sample.

Ellie occupied the hour's drive to San Antonio plotting how best to rush through a DNA test. Jack expressed far more interest in obtaining the blood test required for a marriage license.

He solved the first problem by swinging by the

federal courthouse. Tracking down the two FBI agents he and Mackenzie had met with the previous day, he traded an update on the Foster situation for a promise to strong-arm their lab into an overnight DNA analysis.

He took care of second problem with a stop at the emergency room where Ellie's cuts had been treated two days ago. Her eyes widened when he pulled into the lot.

"Jack! You were serious? You really want to get married right away?"

"This afternoon, if we can talk the doc into doing the blood work and track down a judge to waive the three day waiting requirement. Why? Are you having second thoughts?"

"No! But my mother, my aunt and uncle... They'll be crushed if we don't invite them."

Jack gave her a wry look. "Your uncle Eduardo, huh?"

"Uncle Eduardo," Ellie said firmly. "He might not be able to rearrange his schedule and fly up here on short notice, but for all his overbearing ways, he's been as much a father to me as an uncle. I have to invite him. And, well..."

She fiddled with the plastic bag holding Josiah Kennett's precious letter. The mere thought of joining her life with Jack's sent excited anticipation racing through her veins. After so many years, so many hurts, the future held all the promise their past had cut short.

Ellie didn't want anything to spoil their day. Anything.

"Let's think about this waiting period. If we work things right in the next twenty-four to thirty-six hours, we can go off on a nice, long honeymoon with no loose ends left dangling."

"Like Josiah Kennett," he said with a smile.

"And Daniel Foster."

Jack kept the smile on his face, but it took some doing. At this point he couldn't say how much, if any, of his urgent need to make Ellie his stemmed from an instinctive, gut-deep desire to give her every protection a man can give his woman. All he knew was that he didn't like the idea of Ellie going head-to-head with Foster. At all!

From all indications, the bastard had arranged the murder of one woman. If pushed to the wall, he might take matters into his own hands. The man was big enough, ruthless enough, desperate enough to pull the trigger if he thought he could get away with it.

Jack would just have to make sure Foster knew he couldn't get away with it.

"All right," he conceded. "We take care of the loose ends, then we get married."

After that, it seemed to Ellie as though events moved with the speed of light.

Anticipating a wedding, preparing a public announcement of a major historical find and rehearsing responses to several different scenarios involving Dan Foster took up the rest of that evening and most of the next day.

RSVPs came pouring in. All the local TV and radio stations were sending crews. The mayor and most of the city council intended to make an appearance. Almost every local member of the Alamo Restoration and Preservation Foundation accepted—including Daniel Foster.

As it turned out, Mackenzie didn't have to place a second call to Foster and inveigle an invitation to be his date. He called her. Listening to the tape of their brief conversation gave Ellie a distinctly queasy sensation. If the man was driven by anything more than a desire to show up with a gorgeous female draped over his arm, he hid it well.

Gorgeous, he'd certainly get. Mackenzie had made good on her promise to do some serious shopping. The midnight blue sheath she displayed to Ellie dipped dangerously low in the front, even lower in back.

Claire, too, had found the perfect gown to complement her silvery blond beauty. The shimmering turquoise silk was strapless, banded with silver sequins at the bodice and split up one side. Ellie had no idea how the woman would hide anything, much less her neat little revolver, under that whisper of silk. Smiling, Claire admitted that a holster strapped to the inside of her thigh made gliding across a room an exercise in extreme care.

Forcefully reminded of her woefully inadequate wardrobe, Ellie coerced the two women into a return trip to the elegant little boutique they'd discovered in River Center mall. Those sixty minutes turned out to be among the most expensive of Ellie's life. She ended up purchasing not only a gown for the reception that night, but a cream-colored silk suit perfect for a wedding, a flame-colored chiffon nightdress that clung to her every curve and lacy underwear designed more for seduction than for comfort.

Mackenzie took one look at the scraps of lace and promptly bought two pair for herself. Even Claire was convinced to splurge on the outrageously extravagant panties.

"Now I really won't be able to walk straight," she said with a rueful smile.

"Maybe not," Mackenzie returned with a grin, "but you'll sure have the colonel wondering why. You notice he hasn't taken his eyes off you since he arrived?"

"As a matter of fact," the psychologist replied serenely, "I have."

The happy saleswoman was ringing up their purchases when a cell phone rang. All four women checked their phones. Ellie flipped hers open.

"Dr. Alazar. Yes, I can hold."

Gnawing on her lower lip, she waited for Janet Dawes-Hamilton to come on the line.

"Ellie?"

"Yes."

"As you requested, the FBI sent me the results of the DNA profile their lab worked up for you. I just ran it against the samples we took from the skeletal remains."

"And?"

"We have a match, girl!"

Whooping, Ellie danced around her startled companions.

The shopping expedition and thrilling report from her colleague succeeded in holding Ellie's nervousness at bay for an all-too-brief hour. It came rushing back when the three women returned to the hotel and got caught up in the flurry of last-minute preparations for the function that night.

Jack insisted Ellie rehearse a variety of different responses for if and when she confronted Foster. The responses ranged from merely smiling and letting Foster do all the talking to dropping facedown on the floor if his hand moved so much as an inch toward his tux or pants pocket. After the third or fourth drop, she was a bundle of raw nerves. Pleading the need to review her speech a final time before dressing, she escaped to her bedroom.

Jack knocked on the connecting door at the time

they'd set as the time to leave the hotel. Ellie had just finished putting the final touches to her makeup. Thankfully, the cuts on her palms had healed enough for her to leave off the bandages. A light application of pancake makeup muted most of the scabs. Fighting a panicky flutter of nerves, she tucked a stray curl into the feathery cluster on top of her head and opened the door.

"Oh, my!"

Nine years ago, she'd taken one look at a tall, broad-shouldered Marine in his dress blues and immediately decided to wrangle an introduction and a dance. When Jack had arrived at the Menger, his rugged informality had at first surprised her, then stirred her senses.

This Jack rocked her on her heels.

His tux might have been cut by the hand of a master. The black broadcloth showcased his broad shoulders. Silver studs winked at the front of his snowy white shirt. A satin cummerbund nipped in his trim waist, and a matching satin stripe ran down the outside of his pants legs. What struck Ellie even more than the elegance of the formal attire was the casual ease with which he wore it.

"Where did you get a tux to fit you on such short notice?" she asked when she recovered her breath.

"Nick had it delivered. Compliments of the same tailor who rigs out his waiters."

If Nick Jensen's employees waited tables in hand-tailored tuxes like this one, it was no wonder dinner at one of his glitzy watering holes reputedly cost more than the down payment on a four-bedroom house.

"You look incredible," Ellie murmured.

"*I* look incredible?"

Jack's glance made a slow journey down her length. Just as slowly, he brought his glinting gaze to hers.

"You're going to have every man in the room tonight wishing they could go back to school and take more history courses."

Ellie had to admit the slinky silver lamé gown was about as far from academia as anything could get. The plunging halter top left her shoulders and back bare, while the pencil-slim skirt clung to her hips and glittered with every step. Paired with the silver bracelet Jack had given her nine years ago and dangly silver earrings, the effect was pure Hollywood.

If she'd had more time to deliberate and less on her mind, she might have chosen something more restrained, more dignified. The gleam in Jack's eyes made her glad she hadn't.

"I have something I want you to wear tonight," Jack said. Sliding his hand into his pocket, he produced what looked like a thin transparent patch.

"What is it?"

"A wireless transmitter, compliments of Mackenzie."

His knuckles warm on the slope of her breast, he stuck the tiny device to the inside folds of the halter top.

"Don't take this off tonight. For any reason."

"I won't."

He hesitated a moment, his fingers lingering on her warm skin before reaching into his pocket once more. This time he produced a little box bearing the logo of the jewelry shop just off the Menger's lobby.

"I was going to wait and let you pick out the ring you wanted, but I saw this downstairs and thought it would match your bracelet."

"Oh, Jack! It's beautiful!"

The diamonds were channel cut and set flush in a narrow platinum engagement ring. A wider wedding ring of beaten platinum nestled in the black velvet below the diamonds. Leaving the wider band in place, he popped the box shut and slipped the diamonds on her finger.

Ellie waggled her fingers, marveling at the fiery sparkle. She couldn't quite believe so much was happening so fast!

"I've got a gift for you, too," she told him. "Nothing near as beautiful as this ring *or* my bracelet, but... Well... Wait here a minute."

Hurrying into the sitting room, she retrieved the silver concho.

"I thought you might like this as a souvenir. It's the concho you found at Mission San Jose."

Pleasure softened his features as he worked his thumb over the intricate design. "Don't you need it to substantiate your findings?"

"Not with Josiah's letter and Dorrie's DNA sampling."

"Then I'll keep it."

Sliding the concho into his breast pocket, he drew her forward. His kiss was long and hard and went a long way to calming Ellie's jittery nerves. The reassuring smile he gave her helped, too.

"Time to go. Are you ready?"

She drew in a shaky breath. "As ready as I'll ever be."

Nick's more than lived up to its reputation.

The restaurant occupied the entire top floor of one of San Antonio's tallest buildings. An outside glass elevator whisked patrons upward while providing stunning views of the Riverwalk and the floodlit Alamo. Guests stepped out of the elevator into an eagle's aerie with a spectacular three-hundred-sixty-degree view of the city. Floor-to-ceiling glass panels stood open to the night to allow easy circulation between the dining area and the mist-cooled balcony.

Ellie had never been to a Nick's, but understood they were famous for incorporating local culture and cuisine. This particular establishment offered the best of Texas with a distinctly Hispanic flavor. Discreetly lighted niches displayed museum-quality pieces of sculpture and art depicting the rich heritage of the area. The wine cellar, she'd been told, stocked some fifteen hundred labels, including a number of rich, hearty Texas reds bottled in Hill County vineyards.

For tonight's bash, the lush greenery that provided diners an illusion of privacy without impeding their view had been removed, as had most of the tables. This was a stand-up reception with an open bar and a lavish spread of hot and cold delicacies, subsidized by the restaurant's owner. Good thing, as Ellie knew the pitiful bit of funding that remained in the project kitty wouldn't have covered the drinks, let alone succulent Gulf shrimp sautéed in a white wine sauce, bourbon seared beef tenderloins, and a *carne asada* with the most delicate, delicious aroma she'd ever sniffed.

A good number of guests in black tie and glittering cocktail dresses and gowns had already assembled. Conversation hummed. Ice clinked in glasses. Tux-clad waiters floated between groups refilling glasses and plates. Her palm clammy where it rested in the crook of Jack's arm, Ellie skimmed a quick glance over the assembled guests in search of Mackenzie and her escort.

Foster had picked Mac up at the hotel twenty minutes ago. Ellie had been kept out of sight, but Nick, Jack, Claire and Colonel Esteban had observed the pickup from different vantage points. Claire and

Luis had trailed the couple in Luis's rented Lincoln. Both couples should have arrived by now.

A fact that obviously played on Nick's mind when he greeted Ellie and Jack.

"Comm's playing her part to the hilt," he informed them. "She managed to talk Foster into a detour on the way here, ostensibly to show her another building he constructed."

Annoyance darkening his blue eyes, Lightning flicked the cuffs of his dress shirt. If the stark black and white of formal dress tamed Jack's rugged good looks, Nick Jensen wore his like he'd been born to them.

"From the tenor of the transmissions we're receiving," he said with something less than his usual urbane charm, "she's succeeded in upping the man's pucker factor by several degrees."

She was certainly upping Ellie's. The delay set her nerves snapping and sparking like downed electrical lines. She longed to snatch one of the crystal champagne flutes from the tray a smiling waiter presented, but she knew she had to keep a clear head.

Instead, she sipped at the glass of Perrier Nick procured for her with a single word to the waiter. The overhead lights shot brilliant sparks off the diamonds on her hand as she lifted the heavy crystal goblet. Nick's glance went to the ring, then to Jack. A smile played at his eyes, but he said nothing.

"There's the mayor," he commented. "As host for tonight's event, I'd better greet him."

"And I should look over the layout for the presentation," Ellie said to Jack.

Nodding, he led her to an area cordoned off by black velvet ropes. Rows of straight-backed chairs emblazoned with a gold N faced a raised platform. A wall-size screen would be lowered from the ceiling behind the podium on the platform.

Gulping, Ellie clutched her little silver lamé evening bag. Inside were a lipstick, a compact and a CD in a thin plastic case. She'd boiled down all her weeks of work, all the hours at the dig and at the Alamo, all her team's collective research into a dramatic slide presentation. It was astounding how much history could be crammed onto a single CD.

Her fingers tightened on Jack's arm. "Do you think I'll actually get to present the findings tonight?"

"Yes. Just play this out the way we rehearsed. Exactly the way we rehearsed."

She felt like a Ping-Pong ball bouncing between the public drama of her presentation and the very private, very tense drama with Foster.

"I just hope the rest of the team arrives in time," she said nervously.

Orin Weaver had made arrangements to fly to San Antonio. Janet Dawes-Hamilton was driving down from Waco. Sam Pierce had indicated he'd show, too, and had coerced the National Park Service regional director into coming with him. Ellie had made sure invitations went to each of the volunteers, as well. The only member of the team she hadn't been able contact was Eric Chapman. The grad student was on the road somewhere between San Antonio and Albuquerque and not answering his cell phone.

If her team was still arriving, most of Jack's was already in place. Nick circulated among the crowd, greeting the mayor and other dignitaries with an ease that astounded Ellie considering the fact that he was also receiving a steady stream of transmissions from his headquarters. She couldn't begin to imagine how he separated the mayor's polite patter from the voices feeding into his right ear.

She spotted Detective Harris on the far side of the room, tugging a finger at the tight black bow tie encircling his neck. Jack had indicated upward of a half dozen more of SAPD's finest would be in attendance tonight. Ellie thought she recognized one of the FBI agents she'd met yesterday. The other was here, as well, but she couldn't see him in the growing crowd.

The media had turned out en masse. Banks of TV cameras stood ready opposite the podium. Reporters with mikes and Minicams vied for space and the best backdrops in the roped-off area reserved for interviews. They understood Ellie and her team wouldn't be available until after the presentation but were managing to capture other VIPs on tape.

"Guess we'd better circulate," she murmured, dragging in a shaky breath. "At least until Mackenzie and her date make an appearance."

They arrived less than ten minutes later. Claire and Luis Esteban drifted in almost on their heels.

Ellie sensed rather than saw their entrance. Jack's arm went taut under hers. The skin pulled tight across his cheeks. Gulping, she saw his eyes narrow as he tracked his prey.

She turned slowly, searched the crowd milling at the entrance for a glimpse of a midnight blue gown. Mackenzie floated into view a second later, clinging like a burr to Dan Foster.

The builder's face was ruddy above his black tie. Even from this distance, Ellie could see the sheen of sweat at his temples. His eyes darting around the restaurant, he dragged a folded handkerchief from his pocket and dabbed his forehead.

Across the room, his gaze locked with Ellie's. His hand froze in mid dab for a second, maybe two. Abruptly, he stuffed the handkerchief in his pocket and turned away.

After so many hours of clawing tension and dread, trapping Daniel Foster in the net he had woven proved embarrassingly easy. Almost anticlimactic.

Mackenzie played her role to perfection. While the entire team watched from various vantage points, she snuggled up to Foster, whispered coyly and did everything but stick her tongue in his ear to add to his obvious edginess.

Nick Jensen, Ellie saw in a quick glance, didn't appear to fully appreciate her performance. Like Jack, he tracked the builder's progress around the room with narrowed eyes.

Foster was obviously searching the crowd, looking for one face in particular, growing more tight-jawed by the moment when he didn't spot it. Since a good number of guests had drifted onto the balcony to enjoy the view, it didn't take much work on Mackenzie's part to steer her escort there, as well. With seemingly effortless ease, she maneuvered him to the corner Jack had chosen earlier. A bend in the building left that particular niche shielded from view of most of those inside. The wrought-iron lampposts scattered around the balcony cast only a dim spear of light in that direction.

It was barely enough to illuminate Mackenzie as she withdrew her arm from Foster's and pantomimed powering her nose. Distracted, he gave a terse nod. A moment later, a stunning figure in midnight blue floated past Ellie and Jack on her way to the ladies' room.

"All right, you two. He's all yours."

Swallowing, Ellie swiped her hand down the sides of her dress. Her damp palms slid over the glittering metallic material. Too late, she realized that she'd left smears of the makeup she'd used to cover the ugly scabs on her hands.

Wondering how in the world she could even *think* about such trivia at a time like this, she started forward.

Jack held her back. "Remember how we rehearsed it. If he lifts so much as a finger, you hit the deck."

"Don't worry! I'll go down like the *Titanic*. Now let's get this over with."

The scene that followed might have been scripted. When Ellie moved into the circle of dim light cast by the wrought-iron lamppost behind Foster, the builder reacted just as Claire had predicted he would.

His eyes turned wary. His shoulders went taut under his tux. But no one watching from more than a few feet away would see anything but affability in his smile.

"Mr. Foster?"

"Yes."

"I'm Elena Alazar. I understand your wife was one of the leading contributors to the Alamo Restoration and Preservation Foundation. I just wanted to say how very sorry I was to hear about her tragic death."

"Thank you."

"I know there's been some concern on the part of other foundation members about my team's findings. I just wanted to assure you that…"

With a show of concern, Ellie took another step

forward. That was as close as she dared get to the man whose knuckles had gone white where his hand gripped the balcony rail.

"Mr. Foster? Are you all right?"

His glance was riveted on something just beyond her. She didn't have to look around to know it was the gleam of a long, lethal silencer.

"Are you crazy!" Foster whispered, frantically searching the shadows behind the gun. "Not here! Not with me standing two feet away from her!"

"Mr. Foster, what in the world? Oh!"

Ellie froze as something hard jabbed into the small of her back.

"Don't make a sound," a deep voice rasped from behind her. "Or a move. One twitch and you're dead."

She didn't have to fake the ice that crystallized in her veins. The press of that gun barrel against her bare skin was all too real. The voice so eerily like the one at the Alamo that Ellie couldn't breathe, much less twitch.

Foster fed on her fear like a jackal feasted on carrion. With a snarl, he pushed away from the railing.

"For Christ's sake, keep her here in the shadows until I get across the room. Then do it right this time and blow the bitch away."

"If I blow anyone away," Jack answered in his own voice, "it'll be you."

His jaw dropping, the builder whirled back. "What the hell…?"

"Take one step." With a savage smile, Jack stepped out of the shadows. "Just one."

The beefy contractor was no fool. He froze right where he was. With a grunt of acute disappointment, Jack raised his voice.

"Did you get that, Comm?"

Mackenzie sailed through the glass door. Nick, Claire, Esteban, Detective Harris and the FBI man crowed right on her heels. Behind them, TV crews scrambled frantically to aim their cameras and lights.

"We all got it," she announced, shooting Foster a look of utter scorn. "I broadcast the murdering bastard live."

Epilogue

Washington, D.C.,'s muggy July had given way to a surprisingly pleasant August when Renegade ushered his new bride up the steps of an elegant town house set halfway down a shady street just off Massachusetts Avenue.

Ellie had already met a good number of Jack's friends and colleagues. Men and women with curious code names like Jaguar, Cowboy, Artemis, Chameleon and Thunder had converged on San Antonio, families in tow, for the wedding that had taken place at Mission San Jose the day after Ellie gave a name and a history to the solitary solider who'd died so many years ago on mission grounds. In addition to that lively group, a whole contingent of Marines showed up unexpectedly. Square-shouldered and spit-shined, they stated emphatically that they had to see their old Gunny take the plunge with their own eyes.

Jack's friends weren't the only ones who crowded into the beautiful old church. Ellie's team had showed up *en masse*. A tall, handsome Marine escorted a beaming Dorrie Johnson to her pew. The First Lady of Mexico and her sister-in-law occupied the front pew on the bride's side.

The media had turned out, too. Dr. Alazar, one was heard to proclaim, sure provided *great* copy. TV Minicams whirred and cameras flashed as the President of Mexico escorted his niece down the aisle.

The wedding supper that evening was held on a string of colorful barges floating along the San Antonio River. Candles winked in crystal chimneys. A mariachi band serenaded the guests. Nick's catered the food and wine. It was, Ellie had decided, the perfect ending to her visit to San Antonio and her quest to discover the identity of a fallen Texas hero.

It was also, she thought on a flutter of pure happiness, the perfect beginning for her new life with her own particular hero. A beginning that included a honeymoon in the Pyrenees, where she intended to entice Jack into exploring the mysteries of some recently discovered ice-age cave paintings.

First, though, he'd insisted on a stopover in Washington. It was time, he'd stated, she understood exactly what he did for a living.

The tour a smiling Nick Jensen gave Ellie of the offices of the special envoy didn't shed any particular light on the subject. Not until he ushered her and Jack into an elevator hidden behind a walnut panel fitted with a titanium insert and whisked her up to Mackenzie Blair's domain did she grasp the significance of that bulletproof shield. The door slid open to reveal a state-of-the-art war room.

"Good grief!" Stunned, Ellie took in digital displays that took up three of the four walls. "What is this? An alternate command center for the Joint Chiefs of Staff?"

"They wish!" Her eyes sparkling, Mackenzie waved a proprietary hand. "Nope, this is all mine."

She caught Nick's hooked eyebrow and made a slight correction.

"*Mostly* mine. Come on, I'll show you around."

Dazed, Ellie was treated to a detailed description of the control center's futuristic array of electronics, a visit to the field dress unit, a view of weaponry at the firing range that would have challenged even the data stored in Discoverer Two, and finally a highly sanitized briefing of OMEGA's charter.

Enough of its mission came through, though, to make her frown and swing around in her chair.

"This is what you do, Jack?"

"It's what I did," he answered quietly. "What I do from here on out depends on you."

Startled, Mackenzie and the other agents present at the briefing flashed a quick look at Lightning. He shook his head, signaling that this was news to him, too.

"I don't want you worrying every time I walk out the door, Ellie, or wondering if I'll come back. I came here today to terminate my membership in this elite club."

Relief washed through her, followed immediately by the sharp sting of regret. She'd cost Jack one career. Now he was giving up another for her. Her smile wobbly, she opted to continue this discussion without an interested audience.

"We'll have two weeks in the Pyrenees. Why don't we talk about it there?"

The wolfish grin that slashed across Jack's face said more clearly than words that his plans for those two weeks didn't include a whole lot of talking. Nodding to the others, he escorted Ellie out of the control center.

Mackenzie folded her arms. Toe tapping, she stood beside Lightning and watched the two leave. She liked Ellie. Liked *and* respected her. But she wasn't happy with the idea Renegade might not rejoin the ranks of active operatives. Mac considered each and every one of them her personal responsibility.

"Do you think he'll really give up OMEGA for her?"

Nick slanted her an enigmatic look. "Wouldn't you, for the right man?"

The glint in his blue eyes closed Mackenzie's throat. She had to take in a quick gulp of air before she could inject the right note of nonchalance into her reply.

"Maybe. Maybe not. Guess I'll just have to wait for the right man to make his move and see what happens."

Nick's amused glance followed her across the control center. "I guess you will," he murmured.

*   *   *   *   *

 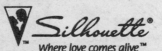

COMING NEXT MONTH